THE PSYCHIC

A Starlight Café Novel

by

Lovelyn Bettison

Nebulous Mooch Publishing

2018

PART ONE

CHAPTER ONE

"WHAT do the cards say?" the redhead asked, leaning forward in her chair.

The coffee shop was nearly empty, having just wound down from the lunchtime rush. A few people sat at the tables, staring at their laptop screens. Many came here to get work done as they nursed a cup of coffee. Cheryl straightened the cards. "The first card reflects your current condition." She pointed to the card showing a woman seated on a throne holding an ornate cup in her hand. "The Queen of Cups."

"That's good, right?" the redhead asked. Her name was Ruth. She worked as a cashier in the coffee shop. Cheryl saw her every day and knew from careful observation what she needed to hear.

Cheryl nodded. "The Queen of Cups is a contemplative card. Notice how she is looking at the cup she holds in her hand. You are going through a stage of looking inward. You are sorting out your thoughts and learning about yourself." She watched Ruth who was drinking in her words. "This is also an intuitive card. You are connecting to your own intuition."

Ruth nodded in agreement. "That's right. I've been doing a lot of reading and thinking these days. I used to go out a lot, but these days I want to stay at home and think. It's weird really because I always hated being alone, but now I crave it."

"You're using this time to reflect and tap into who you are. It's necessary right now."

"This probably sounds weird, but I used to hardly spend any time alone because it was scary. I didn't like myself much, so I didn't want to have to spend time alone thinking, but that's all changed. I don't know if it's because I'm getting older or what?"

Cheryl chuckled. Ruth was only twenty-one. "That's good."

"It's like I'm becoming a completely different person. In a good way, you know." She was so happy to tell Cheryl this and Cheryl couldn't help but smile. She loved reading tarot because she liked to help people get insights into their lives and who they were.

Cheryl had gotten her first tarot card reading in college. The solemn girl who lived in the room next to hers had spread out the cards in front of Cheryl in the dining hall. The girl had hardly spoken to Cheryl before that day but had sat next to her out of the blue and told her she could predict her future. Fascinated, Cheryl agreed to the reading. The cards interested her more than anything the girl had said. She liked the artwork, and soon realized even though they had specific meanings, in her mind she could make them mean anything. She bought a deck of her own from a small store that sold incense and crystals. Before the week was over, she was already doing readings for herself, studying the pictures, and interpreting them for her own life. Then she started giving her roommate readings and her roommate's friends. The cards had a certain power Cheryl lacked in her own life. It was strange how people who would normally ignore her listened when the message came from the cards. Cheryl always wanted to help people, and the cards gave her a way to do that. She told them what they thought was true but needed to hear from someone else. She helped them make hard decisions and face problems they'd been trying to bury for years.

She had watched Ruth for weeks now. She knew Ruth was an optimistic girl who liked music and had a tendency to dance as she rang up customers. She laughed loudly at people's jokes but had an unexpected shy streak. She had a crush on one of the regulars. Cheryl could tell by the way she twisted her hair and leaned in whenever he spoke to her. The young man who was the subject of her affections liked Ruth too but was too shy to make a move. He grew flush whenever they spoke. Cheryl delighted at the idea of the two of them together.

"There is love in your future," she said, motioning to another card.

This interested Ruth. Her eyes widened, and a grin crept across her face. "When?"

Love was a favorite subject among her clients. Cheryl knew when a reading wasn't going well, all she had to do was mention love to get things back on the right track. Most of them had problems with love. Cheryl understood that because her luck with love wasn't exactly great either. She'd only been with one man in her life and had let him hurt her in ways that no one should.

"You will develop a romantic relationship with someone you already know." Cheryl paused and squinted down at the cards. She often did this for dramatic effect. "He could be a friend or someone you know from work."

Ruth inhaled sharply. "I can't believe this."

"Do you have any idea who I'm talking about?"

Ruth looked around the coffee shop, then turned back to Cheryl. She slapped the dark wooden table with her palms. "There is a customer who comes in every day. I like him a lot. It might not be him, but I'm hoping."

This was exactly what Cheryl expected to hear. "He's interested in you too, but he's a little shy." Cheryl felt free to fill in the gaps when the cards did not. She'd always done that. She was guided by more than what the cards showed. If asked, she had a hard time explaining, but sometimes she knew more than the cards could tell her and more than she could observe. Admittedly, this wasn't one of those times. Anyone could see the young man liked Ruth too.

"I thought he might, but I wasn't sure. Do you think I should make the first move?"

"That's what the cards are saying." It was as if Cheryl could see the cogs turning in Ruth's head as she imagined herself asking her crush out.

"I could do that. I mean, I'd be nervous, but I could do it if I knew he wouldn't reject me."

So many of Cheryl's clients wanted to know for sure

before they did anything, but she couldn't make any promises. "I'm only telling you what the cards are telling me. It is up to you to act upon it."

"Ruth, your break is over," the manager called from behind the counter.

Ruth stood quickly. "Thanks. I have to get back to work." She reached into the pocket of her jeans and pulled out a wad of cash. "This should be enough," she said, handing it to Cheryl without counting it.

Cheryl smoothed out the money and counted it as Ruth hurried through the shop and took her place behind the register. Cheryl remembered the first time someone paid her to read their cards. She was sitting outside the library on her college campus. It was a balmy spring afternoon. The pale-green leaves on the tree rustled with the energy of renewed life. Cheryl was giving herself a reading when one of the professors sat down on the picnic bench across from her. The professor let out an exasperated sigh and ran her fingers through her short graying hair before saying, "Do the cards say life will get any easier for me?"

Cheryl knew she was a literary arts professor. Many of Cheryl's classmates loved her, but Cheryl had never taken a class from her. She'd also heard the professor's mother, whom she'd spent many years caring for, had recently died. "Come sit next to me, and we'll find out," Cheryl had said, scooting over on the bench.

She shuffled the deck as the professor took a seat beside her. She didn't remember exactly what she'd told the professor during the reading. She knew she was reassuring, telling her she could overcome anything, and her mother was still with her. After the reading, the professor wiped the tears from her eyes before pulling out her wallet and handing Cheryl a twenty-dollar bill.

"I can't take this," Cheryl said, holding the money out to the professor.

"You already did," the professor said, walking away across the bright green grass.

That was the first time Cheryl realized she could charge to read tarot cards. It didn't take long for her to get the manager of the shop she'd bought the cards from to let her do readings there twice a week. She always made sure to dress the part of a fortune teller, or at least what she thought a fortune teller would look like. She'd let her ebony curls fall loosely around her shoulders instead of wearing them in the ponytail she sported daily on campus. She bought long gauzy skirts and white billowing shirts. She stacked bangles on her wrists that clanked every time she moved her hands. She'd sit in the back corner of the shop waiting for someone to show interest in her. Most customers didn't. They browsed the crystal jewelry and sniffed packs of incense. When the occasional customer wandered to the dark corner where Cheryl sat, she was eager to read their cards. She'd jump to her feet and rush to introduce herself. She scared quite a few potential clients off with her awkward conversation and tendency to ramble, but the few people she managed to read for were always pleased.

Cheryl was a pleaser. That was what drew her to this work. Graduating from school and realizing no one wanted to hire a philosophy major kept her in it. She never imagined she would be a tarot card reader when she graduated, but she managed to eke out a modest living reading in boutiques and coffee shops. When her business slowed, she would work for a psychic hotline. Business had started winding down for Cheryl recently, and she was scheduled for one of her first shifts in a long time on the Spirit Guides Hotline. She looked up at the clock on the wall opposite her. She would need to log into the system in two hours.

She knew the probability of getting another client when the coffee shop was this empty was low, so Cheryl decided to go home. She strolled over to the counter made of dented, dark, reclaimed wood and waited to get the barista's attention. The barista had a short, blonde pixie cut and a silver nose ring. Her black and white striped dress clung to her delicate frame. Upon finishing making a cappuccino for a plump man in a dark gray suit the barista looked over at Cheryl.

"Do you need something?" she asked.

"Can I get a large soy latte to go?" Cheryl said.

The barista turned to Ruth and belted out, "Ring up a large soy latte."

"My drinks are on the house." Cheryl had made an arrangement with the owner when she started doing readings at the Starlight Café. This barista was new and didn't know her.

The barista looked at Ruth for confirmation and Ruth nodded her head. "Sorry, nobody told me," she said to Cheryl.

"No problem." Cheryl watched her make her drink. The barista moved quickly. She didn't have to think about what she was doing even though she was new there. She put the drink on the counter, and Cheryl asked, "What's your name?"

"Sarah," the barista said.

"You're good at what you do."

"You haven't even tasted your latte yet." Sarah nodded toward the creamy drink on the counter in the white paper cup. A white heart floated in the foam on top.

"I don't need to taste it. I can tell by how effortlessly you move when you make it." Cheryl put the cup to her lips and slurped up her smooth milky drink. "Perfect," she said, soy milk clung to her upper lip.

Sarah smiled and handed her a napkin. "You'll need this."

"Thanks." Cheryl decorated her drink, adding a bit of brown sugar and a sprinkle of cinnamon. She meandered slowly back to the table where she did her readings, sunk down into the chair, and started stacking up her tarot cards. She had returned them to the box when a tall bookish man in round, tortoiseshell glasses approached her table. He wore a light blue long-sleeved button-down shirt loosely tucked into a pair of black trousers. The shirt was oddly creased on one side almost as if he had been napping. His chestnut brown hair was slightly tousled.

Cheryl had seen this man before. He was a regular. Three times a week he would come into the Starlight Café at about twelve forty-five in the afternoon. He always wore a long-sleeved button-down shirt and dress pants. He would set up his laptop on the bar near the counter. He always sat with his back to Cheryl, so she could see what he was doing on his computer. He played chess for about an hour while he drank one cup of black coffee and ate a ham and cheese croissant sandwich.

Cheryl noticed him because he was good-looking in an intelligent kind of way. She wondered what he did. He seemed to be good at chess because every time she glanced at his computer screen, he was winning.

When he approached the table, Cheryl stood.

"Are you finished for the day?" he asked.

"I was just packing up, but if you want a reading, I have time." She had wanted to give him a reading ever since the first day she saw him. It would be the perfect excuse to talk to him.

"Okay then." He walked around the table and sat down in the chair next to Cheryl's.

"I'm Cheryl." She extended her hand to him to shake.

"Nice to finally meet you, Cheryl. I've seen you so often, but never introduced myself." He shook her hand.

Cheryl waited for him to say his name, but he didn't. "You still haven't."

"What?" he asked.

"Introduced yourself."

"Oh, right. I'm Adam."

"You're quite a chess master, Adam. I hope you don't think this is a violation of your privacy, but I can see your games from here pretty clearly. You win a lot."

He blushed. "I lose a lot too."

"You must be pretty smart because I can't figure out chess to save my life. My uncle used to try to teach me to play, but it wasn't my thing. I'm more of a checkers kind of gal. It's so much easier. You don't have to think about all the different ways different pieces have to move. In checkers, they all do the same thing. Well, unless it's a king, then you can move the piece all kinds of ways. I'm sure you know that already." She watched him for confirmation and when he nodded she continued. "To be honest, I don't really like games. I'd rather read a good book or watch a movie. I'm reading a great crime thriller these days. I read half of it last night. I can't remember the author's name because I'm terrible with names, but the book is called Midnight. Have you heard of it?"

"I don't read much." He looked at her silently, and she stared back at him.

Cheryl liked his face, the square jawline, and the way the skin around his eyes crinkled when he smiled. Dark stubble dotted his chin. His eyelids drooped slightly like he hadn't gotten a good night's sleep. "You're kind of like a cross between an anchorman and a computer nerd," Cheryl heard herself saying. She was thinking that but didn't mean to say it aloud. "I mean if Superman and Lois Lane had a baby it might look like you." That still didn't come out right. Cheryl knew she should probably shut up and get to the reading, but she was bad at shutting up.

"I think they did have a baby."

"I don't know. I don't follow comic books."

"Neither do I," he said.

"You're not as nerdy as I thought then." Cheryl wondered why she was still talking.

He glanced down at the deck of cards. "Are you going to do the reading?"

"Of course ..." She blinked at him blankly trying to recall his name.

"Adam."

"Right. Adam." She repeated it a few times in her head to make sure she remembered. "Do you have a particular question you want answered?"

He nodded. "There is something terrible in my life right now. I need to know how to get rid of it."

She handed him the cards. "Think about your question as you shuffle the cards."

He fumbled with the deck for a few moments before handing it back to her.

"You don't have a future as a blackjack dealer that's for sure," Cheryl joked.

"I've never known what to do with a deck of cards besides put them in my bicycle spokes." He smiled.

"You have cards in your bicycle spokes?"

"I did as a kid."

Cheryl gave a little laugh. "Why do little boys do that?" She remembered the boys that lived up the street from her as a child riding around on their bikes with playing cards in their tires. Dirt smudged on their faces; they'd screech as they rode mimicking the sounds of explosions.

"To make your bike sound like a motorcycle."

"Of course." She placed the deck on the table and had him cut it three times before fanning the cards out on the table in front of them. "Pick a card while thinking about your question."

He chose his card carefully, hovering his hand over one card and then another before making a final decision. This fascinated Cheryl. He was taking the idea of the reading so seriously. She'd thought he'd treat a reading more like a game, something silly to do to pass the time. She got a lot of clients like that who got their cards read on a lark. When he'd chosen his card, she set it face up on the table. While thinking of him and his question, she laid the rest of the spread around that first card.

"Each card represents something in your life." She pointed to the first card, an armored skeleton seated on a white horse. The death card didn't have to be bad, but Cheryl hated when it was the first card any client got during a reading because it scared everyone.

"That can't be good," he said.

"This is the death card, but don't freak out. It can represent a big change in your life. Something will end soon, but when one thing ends something new can begin."

"It doesn't just represent death?" he asked.

She shook her head. "The cards aren't that literal."

"Even when they should be?"

She turned her gaze from the card to him. "Are you dying?" she asked.

"No, but death is following me."

"What do you mean?"

He shifted in his chair and lowered his voice when he spoke. "I think it's safe to assume that because you do this," he motioned to the cards, "you believe in spirits and ghosts and stuff like that."

Cheryl didn't believe in any of those things until she'd started reading people's cards. She didn't even believe in the cards. Doing readings made her more aware of the unseen world. She'd heard so many stories from clients and other psychics that she'd come to believe in the paranormal; even if she never saw evidence of it herself. "You can safely assume that."

"Ever since I moved here I've been haunted. At first, I thought it was the house I was renting. It was an old place in the Old Northeast. I was hearing things and seeing shadowy figures moving around my living room at the edges of my field of vision. I broke the lease and got out, but I'm having a similar experience in my new place. It's a new building right downtown. I wouldn't think it would be haunted. I've been dealing with this for about a year, and I can't seem to get rid of the ghosts. I'm starting to think it's not the buildings that are haunted but me." He looked into her eyes a bit longer than felt comfortable. "Is that even possible?"

"I don't know. I only read the cards." She looked down at the cards spread out on the table. "I don't know anything about hauntings."

"Surely in your line of work you must know something."

She shook her head.

"To be honest, I'm not interested in getting my cards read. I want to get rid of this ghost or whatever it is that's hanging out at my place. It makes it hard to get work done. I don't feel good when I'm alone there. When I tell people, they think I'm crazy, but I swear there is something going on." He spoke quickly.

"I don't think you're crazy. There are spirits all around us. I just don't think I can help you with that beyond what the cards have to say. Should I continue with the reading?"

His shoulders slumped. "Go ahead. Tell me about the next card."

Cheryl continued with the reading trying her best to be as helpful as possible, but she was painfully aware of his disappointment as she spoke. He didn't want to hear what the cards said about his life. He wanted help with something different entirely. He wanted her to help him solve a problem she had no idea how to fix. The reading was optimistic and would've given any other client a renewed sense of hope, but when she finished, Adam didn't look hopeful at all.

"Do you know anyone who exorcises ghosts?" he asked.

"I might be able to recommend someone. I'll have to ask around though."

He frowned and took her business card from the stack that sat at the front of the table.

Cheryl hated to see a client leave unhappy. "Give me your number, and I'll call you when I find someone who can help." She picked up her large quilted purse from the floor and started fishing for a pen. She had a lot of hard caramels, her lucky rock, a bottle of lotion, loose change, a lollipop, and even a whistle, but no pen. "Let me get a pen to write it down."

"Just put it in your phone." He pointed at her cell phone sitting next to the stack of cards on the table.

"I'd rather write it down."

He went over to the bar and wrote his number down on a notepad he had next to his laptop. "Here." He handed the paper to her. "I don't know why you insist on doing it the old-fashioned way."

"I'm just an old-fashioned kind of girl." Cheryl glanced at the number before folding the paper and putting it into her purse.

"If you stick it in there you'll never see it again," Adam said.

"That's not true. I'll call you."

"If you don't, I'll call you." He pulled his wallet from his pocket and stuck her card in before taking out some money to pay her. She held up her hand. "You weren't happy with the reading. I won't take your money."

"Your reading was fine. I'm just distracted these days." He thrust the money toward her.

"I'd rather not take it."

"Please, take it. I'll feel bad if you don't."

Cheryl took the money from him and put it in her wallet. She watched as he slunk off to the bar and started packing up his laptop. She had to get home to start her shift on the Spirit Guides Hotline, but she wasn't going to forget about Adam or his ghost.

"I'll call you as soon as I find someone who can help you," she said to him before leaving the coffee shop.

He gave her a weak smile as she left. Walking home, she couldn't stop thinking about Adam. She'd finally gotten the chance to talk to him. She knew his name. She read his cards, but it wasn't enough. She had to do more.

CHAPTER TWO

ADAM didn't expect the tarot card reader at the coffee shop to be able to help him, but it was worth a try. Ever since she'd started doing readings at the table in the back corner of the Starlight Café he'd been curious about her. So many people seemed to approach her for a reading. He had no idea that many people believed in psychics. She would lay out the cards before them and begin to talk. Sometimes, he could see her in the reflection in his computer screen. Her inky dark hair cascaded over her shoulders. She liked decorative scarves. She'd wear them looped around her throat or tied on her head, sometimes like a turban, and other times like a headband. Sometimes, she wore them knotted around her hips emphasizing the way they swayed when she walked. She wore too many bracelets that jingled like bells every time she moved her arms. Her deep-set eyes and tan skin made him wonder where her ancestors came from, but he'd never ask her that. He'd made that mistake with an ethnically ambiguous coworker once and got an earful. She'd told him that she was American and anything beyond that was none of his business. He hadn't known a simple question could be considered so offensive.

Even though he wanted to, he didn't ask the psychic that, but he did tell her about the ghosts. Telling someone was a relief because ever since it started, he hadn't really been able to tell anyone. He'd kept quiet about it and avoided his apartment by putting in more overtime at work and going out in the evenings. He was getting to the point where he was only at home to sleep, and he didn't do much of that.

He sat at the bar in the modern speakeasy across the street from his work, nursing a beer, and trying to figure out what to do next. It was nine thirty on a Thursday evening. All his coworkers had gone home to their families. Adam had to get up early and knew he should probably head home too.

The bar was still pretty crowded. People knocked against him as they made their way over to order drinks from the bartender, a stick-thin woman in a white, button-down shirt, and black slacks. Her tangerine-orange hair was pinned up in a messy bun. "Can I get you anything else?" she said, noticing he was getting close to the bottom of his glass.

"I could use a good exorcist," Adam said.

She leaned in, straining to hear him over the buzz of the crowd. "What, now?"

He regretted making the joke in the first place because now he would have to repeat it. "I said I could use a good exorcist."

"I don't know that drink. What's in it?" Her voice was raspy.

Adam shook his head. "An exorcist. You know, someone who casts out demons."

She widened her blue eyes at him and gave a little laugh throwing back her head. "I think you might have to go to the Catholic church for that."

A man, with spiky blond hair wearing an "I love New York" T-shirt, motioned at her from the other end of the bar, and she hurried over to get his order.

Adam downed the last of his drink. Numb from the alcohol, he stood just as the bartender returned. "You know someone who's possessed or something?" she asked.

The classic rock that had been blaring from the overhead speakers stopped, making it easier for them to talk. The jazz trio who had been playing all night returned to their instruments.

"No." There was no way for him to talk about what was going on in his apartment without seeming a bit crazy. The best solution was to give short answers and avoid her further inquiries, but she wouldn't let it go.

"Why else would you need an exorcist?"

"I don't really need one. I was joking."

"It wasn't very funny." She turned and walked over to the other end of the bar.

He pushed his empty glass away from him before turning to fight his way through the crowd. The band began to play a song he didn't recognize, but the gentle rise of the music suited the atmosphere of the bar. It was like stepping back in time.

Adam used to prefer silence to music. It gave him space to think, but since ghosts started bumping around his apartment, he sought out sounds to distract himself from the unexplained bumps and crashes.

He didn't live far from work. He liked it that way because he could get most anywhere by bicycle or on foot. It was a chilly night. The wind whipped between the buildings and Adam found himself wishing he'd brought a jacket with him. He didn't have far to walk though. Stuffing his hands into his pockets, he started home. He passed only a few people as he ambled through the streets. He wondered if any of them were living with ghosts too. There was no way to know. He was sure that no one around him suspected the insanity he endured at home. He hid it well, but lack of sleep was catching up with him. He couldn't keep it all a secret much longer. He'd crack soon. He could feel himself coming undone. That's why he saw the psychic. She was his last desperate attempt to get rid of this thing once and for all. At this point, he felt like she was the only psychic in town he hadn't yet asked for help. None of them could do anything for him. Not even her.

He'd left the light on in the entranceway. The amber glow from the copper lamp on the shelf by his front door pushed away the darkness. He always left this light on, so he wouldn't stumble on anything as he came inside. There was a lot he could stumble on. Since moving into this apartment almost a year ago, Adam hadn't been able to get a handle on his life. Boxes yet to be unpacked still lay strewn around. They cluttered the walkways and tabletops. His clothes lay in heaps, and dishes of varying degrees of uncleanness stared at him longing to be washed. He took his wallet and his keys from his pocket and set them on top of the cabinet next to the lamp. This cabinet was the only flat surface in his apartment he'd managed to keep tidy. He always put his keys, wallet, and phone there when he went inside because in any other place they would get lost among the clutter. He turned on the overhead light in the living room and white light washed over the space. In his mind, he could see past the junk and remember what the room would look like if only it were clean. A black leather couch sat against the opposite wall flanked by two simple mahogany end tables. A brown-and-maroon Oriental style rug lay on the dark hardwood floor in front of the sofa with a glass top coffee table centered on it. The eggshell white walls were neglected and bare. He had framed black-and-white photographs he intended to hang on them when he got the chance. They were leaning against the wall in the hallway near the bathroom door. He didn't usually live like this, but with all he'd been experiencing it made it difficult to organize his life. At work, he managed to focus on the job. There was a lot to keep his mind busy there, but when he got home he could only wonder about what was happening to him. His mind was so occupied with what might happen next, he could hardly function.

Even with the light saturating every space in the room, Adam felt like he couldn't see enough. He wanted to be able to look into every nook and cranny and make sure nothing sinister lingered there. He walked through the living room to the bedroom and turned on another overhead light, this one even brighter than the last. He paid close attention to every sound and movement as he got ready for bed.

The previous night had been particularly bad. He'd awoken with a crushing feeling on his chest unable to move. Shadowy figures slunk across the walls, and he tried to cry out for help, but his throat made no sound.

He no longer looked forward to sleep like he once did. As he lay down resting his head on the pillow, he said a silent prayer he would sleep undisturbed through the night. It never took him long to drift off, but it was those wakeful hours in the darkness before sunrise that worried him. "Good night," he said to the dark, empty space around him. "Don't bother me tonight. I have a lot to do in the morning." He fell asleep. As soon as he did a dream caught him. He knew this dream well because he'd had it many times since the haunting started. Jazz rose around him as he weaved through a crowd of people. The women wore bright floor-length dresses and the men were all in black and white. Cigarette smoke hung in the air. Adam was trying to get outside. He needed air, but there was a woman following him. She didn't want him to go. She reached out, grabbing his arm in her cool hand. Adam turned to look at her. She wore her brown hair in a bob that cupped her sharp chin. Her dark, sunken eyes pleaded with him. The woman moved her mouth, but no sound came out. She turned her head looking back toward the party, the people laughing and dancing. Adam saw a chunk of flesh missing from the side of her head. A wound, black and weeping, sat next to her ear.

Adam jolted awake to the hollow sound of water striking the bottom of the bathtub. The bathroom door was closed, and light seeped through the crack beneath it. Adam swallowed hard. He swung his legs out of bed, his bare feet nestling into the thick carpet. His heart thumped as he stood and padded to the door. "Hello?" he called, knowing anything he said was useless. "Is someone there?" He took hold of the doorknob and tried to twist it, but it was locked. "It's the middle of the night. I need to get some sleep." To anyone else, it might've seemed strange trying to rationalize with a ghost, but this was happening so often now that all he could do was try to rationalize. He hoped to be able to talk some sense into this being, so he could get on with his life. This wasn't the first time he had awoken in the night to the sound of the shower, and it probably would not be the last. The shower turning on, the sink filling with water, the toilet flushing; little things like that didn't bother him so much. What bothered him was when it made contact with him, shoving him from room to room, holding him down in bed, sending a chill through him so sharp it seemed to cut his insides.

"I'm tired." He spoke to the bathroom door. "I need to sleep. Knock it off." He tried the doorknob again. This time it turned. The door clicked as it unlatched, and he pushed it open.

Steam billowed out of the bathroom. He walked through it and pulled the shower curtain open. The shower was empty. He wasn't sure what he would've done if it wasn't. He looked around the bathroom. Nothing seemed out of the ordinary. Exhausted, he turned off the light and went back to bed.

Adam remembered the day this all started. He was

renting a one-bedroom bungalow on a tree-lined brick street. It was just under one thousand square feet. The first time he saw the house he knew he wanted to rent it before he even went inside. It felt like family. If only he'd known.

He'd gone to work as usual, and when he came back home, he stuck his key in the front door. It unlocked easily, but when he went to push the door open, the chain lock was on from the inside. The door would only open a crack before the chain stopped it. He assumed a thief was in the house and went running around to the back door expecting to see someone fleeing across the freshly mowed yard. When he got there, he saw no one. He approached the back door slowly and tried the knob. It was locked. He unlocked it with his key, flung the door open and charged inside yelling, "Get out of my house." No one was there. He went from room to room checking the closets, the shower, under the bed ... no one. Nothing in his house was missing. Except for the chain being on the door, everything was untouched. Thinking his new landlady might have been in the house to fix the loose hinge on a cabinet door in the kitchen he'd complained about, he called her. She picked up after the first ring.

"Did anyone come to the house today to fix the cabinet door?" he asked.

"No," she said flatly. "I'll get it fixed before the week is over."

"There's no hurry. I just thought someone was here because the chain was on the door when I came home."

"What do you mean?" Suddenly the call interested her.

"Just what I said. The chain was on the front door. I

went out the front door when I went to work this morning. There was no way I could've put the chain on it." Adam remembered going down the front steps to his car which he'd parked at the curb. Alley access was listed as a positive feature when he rented the house, but Adam didn't like the idea of parking in an alley.

"Is anything missing?" she asked.

"Nothing seems to be." He scanned the rooms one last time to be sure.

After talking to his landlady, he called the police to report an intruder, but when he told the person on the other end of the phone nothing had been stolen from his house her interest waned. No one came to investigate.

That evening he sat in the living room and tried to remember putting the chain on the front door and leaving out the back. It would've been the only possible reason for the state of the house when he got home. He'd almost convinced himself that was what had happened when he saw a dark figure hovering at the far end of the living room in the doorway to the hallway. "Hey," he called out as he rushed toward it. When he got to the doorway, there was nothing there. He saw the figure a few times that night. It appeared to be a thin man with long limbs and a narrow head, but it was difficult to tell what it was exactly. He lay awake that night wondering if he was losing his mind. In the morning he called the landlady again.

"Is this house haunted?" he asked as soon as she picked up the phone.

She laughed. "You have to be kidding."

"I'm not. I want to know. Did anything bad happen

here?"

She was silent on the other end of the phone. "Not that I know of." She finally answered. "You're not going to try to get out of your lease by claiming the house is haunted, are you?"

Adam took a deep breath. What was he doing? He was acting like a teenage girl who'd just used a Ouija board for the first time. "No," he said, but three months later he would successfully get out of the lease. He kept the whole business about the ghosts to himself and made up a bogus reason for moving. Luckily, his landlady found someone else to move into the house right away and was willing to let him off the hook. When he found the new apartment right in the heart of downtown, he was thrilled. He thought there was no way such a new place would have ghosts. He was wrong.

On his first day in his new apartment, the haunting picked up where it had left off in the previous house. He came home one night from work to find all his curtains tied in knots. At first, he tried to pretend it wasn't happening again. He had to stay. There was no way of getting out of this lease. So, he resigned himself to living with the ghost. He could live with his furniture being rearranged when he came home or the water suddenly turning on. He could live with the massive changes of temperature in his house when the ghost decided to adjust the thermostat.

He wasn't sure if it was because it was being ignored, but one day the ghost started touching him physically. That's when he decided he could no longer live with it. The first time it happened, he was in the bathroom shaving. The radio was on. He was singing along and even dancing a little when something nudged him in the middle of his back. It wasn't very hard at first, just a little bump like someone trying to get by him in a crowded place. He turned and looked behind him and saw nothing. He went back to shaving thinking he was imagining things, but it happened again. This time it was harder, making him fall forward. He nicked himself, a bead of blood forming on his chin. He spun around, his heart thumping in his chest.

He finished shaving his face in the kitchen. The bathroom felt too crowded for him. Every cell in his body was on the alert waiting to feel something else unusual, the graze of a hand or wind of hot breath on his neck. Being on edge in his own home was exhausting. When nothing happened for days, he started to relax thinking that nudge was the ghost's way of saying goodbye. He started spending more time at home, assured it was all over until it shoved him across the living room one Saturday evening.

He didn't dare tell anyone in his life what was happening to him. He was a logical guy who worked in the tech department in a growing startup. He didn't believe in ghosts or fairies or anything else supernatural. Even as his beliefs changed because of what was happening in his life at home, he kept it a secret from everyone. He clandestinely hired paranormal investigators and psychics, hoping they would be able to stop all of this. They weren't. Asking the psychic in the Starlight Café was a last-ditch effort. He was hoping she'd have the answers. She didn't, and Adam didn't know what he should do next.

CHAPTER THREE

CHERYL looked at the spread of cards on the coffee table and shook her head. She could hear the measured breathing of her client on the other end of the phone. She adjusted her headset as she tried to decide what to say. Sometimes she wished the cards would come up differently. There was always the temptation to lie when she did her reading over the phone, especially when she felt like she knew exactly what the client needed to hear, but the cards weren't cooperating.

Cheryl wasn't sure if true psychics existed. If they did, it would've been good to be one. She could only do so much with tarot cards and asking questions. She wanted desperately to be able to do more. Most people came to her looking for certainty she couldn't give.

She closed her eyes and took a deep breath before diving into the reading, telling the person on the other end of the phone exactly what the cards told her. This would be her last phone reading of the day.

"Thank you," the woman on the other end of the

phone said when Cheryl finished the reading. "I know what I have to do."

"What's that?" Cheryl asked, afraid of the answer she'd get.

"I have to stay with him for the kids. It'll get better. He'll stop."

Cheryl's heart sank. "No, it won't."

"What do you mean? You just said the cards told me a change would come into my life. That means he'll change. He'll stop. He told me he would."

The cards were open to interpretation. Everything in life was, and Cheryl knew this interpretation was wrong. She'd experienced it before. She married young, younger than she should've to a man who solved problems with his fists. She didn't like the violence, but she could put up with it until it was directed at her.

"They always say that." She hesitated. "My ex-husband used to hit me too. I know what it's like. The first time he did I couldn't believe it was happening. We were arguing and the next thing I knew he punched me in the face. I fell to the ground. I was too shocked to cry or scream or do anything at all. No one had ever hit me before. From the look on his face, he was surprised too. He started apologizing immediately. He said it was an accident, and I wanted to believe him. He bought me flowers the next day and took me out to dinner. He was so nice for a whole month, but it did happen again. It kept happening over and over, and it was worse every time. I started to expect it. That's never a good place to be.

"He never changed. It was hard to leave. I loved him

even though he hit me. Eventually, I had to face reality. I had to admit I was being abused." It was still hard for Cheryl to admit. She liked to think of herself as strong and able to stand up for herself. She did in every other aspect of her life until she was married to him. "It was so hard to leave. I did it though."

"Good for you." The woman's voice shook. "Did you have kids?"

"No, but you can't let your kids stop you. They should motivate you to get out sooner. You don't want your girls to think this is the way a man is supposed to treat a woman. You have to get them out while they are young." Cheryl's own parents had a violent relationship. They would yell and chase each other around their house with steak knives. It was like they took turns beating each other. Each of them grew more insane as time passed.

"I don't have anywhere to go."

Cheryl picked up her laptop from the coffee table. "You're calling from Baltimore. Is that where you live?"

"Yeah."

She did a quick internet search and found several organizations that helped battered women. She gave the woman the telephone numbers.

"The idea of leaving terrifies me."

"But your reading said you have more courage than most, remember?" She waited for the woman to say something, but when she didn't Cheryl continued to speak. "The cards did say a big change will come into your life, but you have to make that change happen. If you keep doing the same things, you'll get the same results. You have to do something different. In this situation, the best change you can make for yourself, your daughters, and even your husband, is to leave."

Muted sobs drifted through the phone.

"Promise me you'll call and make arrangements to leave him."

"I will. You're right. I don't want my daughters to grow up like this. I try to think they don't know, but that's impossible. They have to know. I can't let them stay here."

"No, you can't. That's why when you hang up from this call you're going to call one of those numbers I gave you."

"Thank you for the reading. You've helped me more than you'll ever know."

"You're welcome." As she hung up, Cheryl hoped the woman really would get help. There was no way for her to know what happened once the phone call was over. She liked to imagine life only got better for everyone she read for during the day, but she knew that wasn't possible.

Her three-year-old tabby, Beau, leaped into her lap and started kneading her thighs with his front paws. He leaned into her abdomen and purred. She stroked his silky head and closed her eyes for a moment. She was tired but had invited a few girlfriends over for dinner later in the evening. She was considering calling and suggesting they eat out when her phone started ringing. It was the landline. She'd gotten it when she started working for the psychic hotline because they didn't let workers use their cell phones to take calls. "That's strange," she said to Beau who was looking up at her with his green eyes. When she was logged out of the psychic hotline system, that phone never rang when she wasn't working. She answered it. "Hello?"

There was silence on the other end. After waiting a few moments, she took it away from her ear and went to hang it up, but before her finger hit the button, she heard something coming from the receiver. She put the phone to her ear again.

"Help us," the voice on the other end said, raspy and cracked.

"Who is this?" Cheryl asked.

"Help us before it's too late." The voice was unlike anything she had ever heard before. It sounded like a squeaky hinge.

"How can I help you if I don't know who you are?" Cheryl asked.

The low moan of the dial tone answered her.

Cheryl hung up the phone and put it back on the charger. "It must've been a prank call," she said to Beau.

He looked up at her and meowed.

Cheryl sat on the sofa listening to the water sloshing around inside the dishwasher her friends helped her load before leaving her apartment. She was glad she didn't cancel. She'd ended up making a simple meal of tomato soup and grilled cheese sandwiches. It wasn't what she was originally planning, but it was all her tired brain could handle. Her friends liked it. The meal reminded them of their childhoods, of footed pajamas and hide-and-go-seek. They dipped the corners of their gooey sandwiches into tomato soup as they exchanged stories of summer vacation and elementary school hijinks. That was one of the many things Cheryl liked about food, how it could trigger feelings from the past. With memories flooding her mind, and her stomach comfortably full, she was content to sit on the sofa listening to the dishwasher. The minutes ticked by. Sleep began to tug at her eyelids. She considered lying down on the sofa and sleeping where she was, but knew she'd regret it in the morning when she awoke with a sore back. She yawned. Raising her arms above her head, she stretched. Every inch of her cried out for sleep. With great effort she pushed herself up, her bare feet sinking into the beige carpet. Fringe danced around the hem of her long skirt as she walked to her bedroom. She separated her hair into two sections as she walked and braided each loosely to get ready for bed.

She was rinsing her face in the sink when she thought she heard something. She turned off the water, so she could listen, and realized it was the phone ringing, the landline again. She grabbed the towel from its rack and dried her face as she walked to the living room. Beau got under her feet sending her tumbling to the carpet. Her knee bumped against the floor, and her first thought was her downstairs neighbors. They complained about her being noisy before. She looked up and noticed the clock in her entertainment center read 10:14. The phone continued to ring. The sound seemed to grow shriller with each passing minute. Cheryl stood. No longer in a hurry to answer the telephone she looked down at her knee and gave it a quick rub with her hand.

She picked up the phone and looked at the screen. She

didn't recognize the number. Reluctantly she decided to answer it.

"Hello?"

Crackling hissed and popped in her ear. "Hello?" The voice came through the phone, timid and juvenile.

Cheryl waited for the person on the other end to say something else. The line continued to hiss at just the right frequency to send chills crawling down her spine.

"Where are you?" the voice asked her, barely audible above the hiss.

"Who is this?" The air conditioner rattled before it kicked on. The hair rose on her forearms.

The hissing on the phone grew in a wave of sound.

"Who is this?" Cheryl asked again. Fear and frustration had overwhelmed her fatigue.

"We need your help," the voice said. "Please." The words dragged out over the crackling.

Cheryl's heart raced. "I can't help you if I don't know who you are."

She listened and thought she could hear a second voice, grumbling beneath the static. She strained her ears trying to make out what it was saying but could only hear disjointed syllables. Just as she thought she could begin to make out a word beneath all the noise, the line went dead.

"Hello?" she said into the phone. She hit the button to hang it up and then the one to answer it again. Holding the phone to her ear, she heard the dial tone. Cheryl hung up and returned the phone to its cradle. The dishwasher stopped running. The house became a cocoon of silence.

She could feel someone's gaze moving over her body.

She turned to look at the window on the wall opposite her. The flowered curtains were opened just a crack. She made her way across the floors and closed them, but even with them closed she felt like she was under surveillance. She crossed her arms over her body holding her torso. Any sense of safety she'd felt seemed to fall away. She'd only gotten a phone call, two phone calls. They were strange, but they shouldn't have made her feel so ill at ease. Cheryl crossed the room again and picked up the telephone. She hit the button to see the number that called her last. It came up on the screen, seven digits that felt so threatening. She swallowed hard and hit the button to call it. She pressed a receiver to her ear and listened to the phone ringing.

"Hello?" a woman answered, her voice thick with sleep.

Cheryl wasn't expecting anyone to answer. She almost hung up but decided against it. "Hi. I'm sorry to wake you, but someone from this number just called me."

"You have the wrong number," the woman said.

"That's not possible. I called the number that just called me. Is someone else there that might've made the call?"

"No one else is here, and I'm trying to sleep. You have the wrong number." The woman hung up.

Cheryl didn't have the wrong number. She knew that for sure. There was no way the phone would've dialed the wrong number on its own. She looked at the number and considered dialing it again, but she didn't. Her bed was still calling for her. Her body yearned for sleep.

Even though she was exhausted, Cheryl spent most of the night staring up at the ceiling and listening to Beau skulk around the house. She left the lamp on in the living room because she had never been a fan of the darkness, the way it clung to everything revealing the sinister side of even the most innocent objects.

The lamplight cascading through her bedroom door as she tried to sleep gave her some comfort but not enough to usher in sleep. Every time she closed her eyes she heard the crackling on the other end of the phone. She heard the eerie voice asking her for help. Who was it? How could she help them?

She wished she could stop herself from worrying about it. She had too many things to worry about already. She knew the morning would come and bring with it a new day. Hopefully, she'd feel better in the sunlight.

CHAPTER FOUR

SHE unfolded the aqua-blue-and-purple tapestry and draped it across the table. Cheryl had only just decided to start using it for work thinking the happy colors on the fabric would enhance her readings. She knew looking the part of a psychic was almost as important as the readings themselves, and the tapestry added to the look.

"That's perfect," the store owner said. She stood back with her arms folded watching as Cheryl arranged crystals and tarot cards on her table. "My customers are going to love this."

This gig was a one-off. Cheryl had met the store owner at the Starlight Café a few months ago. She wanted to do something special in her store to celebrate the five-year anniversary of its opening and had decided to pay Cheryl to spend the day giving her customers free tarot card readings. Cheryl wasn't sure she fit into the store with its expensive designer dresses and classical music coming through the sound system. She was more accustomed to places that sold crystals and smelled of incense and sage.

"I hope they do," Cheryl said. "I'm looking forward to doing some interesting readings today."

"I'm sure you'll have a line of people wanting you to tell them what the future has in store." The owner, Roxanne, was so structured looking. Her hair was always pulled up into a neat bun. Her heels were higher than any Cheryl could manage herself, and her tight pencil skirt made her steps small and mincing. She was a regular at the Starlight Café.

The first time Cheryl talked to her, Roxanne had come over to her table in the coffee shop and stood watching her give someone else a reading. Cheryl stopped the reading to ask if she needed something, and when she did Roxanne shook her head and sat down at a table near her. Her presence made Cheryl a little nervous because she could tell Roxanne was still listening to what she was telling her client, a young man with an afro that stood almost a foot high. She wanted to tell Roxanne to give them some privacy but asking for privacy while sitting in the middle of a café seemed a bit ludicrous. People probably listened in to the readings she gave all the time, but most people weren't as obvious as Roxanne. She listened in to a few of the readings before finally deciding to talk to Cheryl.

When Roxanne approached her, Cheryl was sure she would ask for a reading, but she didn't. She asked Cheryl if she wanted to set up in her boutique for a day. It was so strange she'd want to hire her without sampling out a reading for herself first.

"Let me read your cards before we get started. It will be a good way to warm myself up." Cheryl looked at the clock. There were still a few minutes before the store was to open.

Roxanne shook her head. "No thanks. I don't need to know about my future."

"No one needs to know, but they all want to know." Cheryl picked up the deck of cards and held them out to her. "Don't you have a question for the cards?"

Roxanne crossed her arms and thought for a moment. Cheryl thought for sure she'd want a reading, but she shook her head again. "I already have my future planned out. I don't need cards to tell me what will happen."

"The universe might have something else planned for you."

"If it does, I don't want to know." Roxanne walked over to a rack with a few dresses on it and started straightening them. When she finally flipped the sign on the front door indicating the store was open, customers started to come in. Cheryl was only expecting to give a few readings that day, but almost everyone who came into the boutique wanted to know what their cards said. She was halfway into her fourth reading when the shrill ring of her cell phone exploded from her purse.

"I'm so sorry," Cheryl said, horrified that in her preparations for the day she'd somehow forgotten to silence her ringer.

"No problem," her client, a pinched-faced woman with bright red lipstick, said. The way she furrowed her brow when Cheryl reached down to silence the ringing told her the woman really did mind. Cheryl couldn't blame her. Her phone going off in the middle of a reading was not at all professional. She didn't bother looking at the number when she turned it off. She didn't have time. She would check it when the day was over.

"That went well," Roxanne said as she turned the sign on the door back over. The final customers had shuffled out of the store with their arms laden with shopping bags.

When Cheryl saw how much money the women spent in the store, she wondered if she'd charged Roxanne too little to do readings in her shop all day. She wasn't good with money, and this was an unusual situation. Normally, the people she gave readings to paid her. She never had to name a single price for an entire day of work. If she were charging the customers for individual readings, she would've made more than twice what she'd asked Roxanne to pay her. It was too late to bring that up, though. She'd made a deal with her and had to keep her word.

"Thanks so much. My customers enjoyed it." Roxanne took an envelope out from under the counter and handed it to Cheryl. "I'll have to have you back some time."

"Yeah," Cheryl said. "Your shop is so popular. I did a lot more readings than I expected."

She stuck the envelope in her bag without checking to make sure the payment was right and left the boutique with her purse slung over her shoulder. She was tired and wanted to get home and get some rest before she started her evening shift on the Spirit Guides Hotline. As she started her walk home, she wished she'd taken her car that morning. She could've done with a few minutes' drive to her house instead of the twenty-minute walk it was going to be. She pulled her phone from her bag to check the time and noticed five missed calls. Scrolling through, she saw they were all from the same unfamiliar number. There was only one message, but after her experiences with unknown numbers the previous day she didn't want to listen to it. She was thinking about whether she'd just delete the message without listening when the phone began to vibrate in her hand. It was the same number calling her again. Part of her wanted to stick the phone in her bag and pretend she didn't know it was ringing, but if the call was as creepy as the others, it was better to answer it on the busy street in the dusty light of the end of the day than at home alone. She stepped to the side of the sidewalk out of the way of passersby and answered the phone. She was never very good at walking and talking on the phone at the same time. Whenever she did she'd always end up bumping into something or someone. Once she almost stepped out in front of a car. That's when she decided she'd only talk on the phone while standing still.

"Hello?" She braced herself for the loud crackling sound and the frightening voice, but that wasn't what she heard at all.

"Cheryl? This is Adam, from the coffee shop."

"Adam, I haven't found anyone who can help you yet. I've been so busy and to be honest, I forgot. That isn't normally like me, but it just kind of happened. Life has been a bit weird lately." Cheryl always tried to keep her word. Admitting that she hadn't even attempted to find someone was embarrassing.

"I had a pretty rough night." He paused for a moment, and Cheryl could hear the clang of cups and the buzz of conversation in the background. She wondered if he was at the Starlight. "The ghost woke me up every few hours," he whispered into the phone. "I might have to stay with a friend tonight."

"I'm sorry. What happened?"

"I don't want to discuss it on the phone. Someone might overhear me and think I'm nuts. Not that I'd blame them. I feel like I'm losing my mind."

"If it makes you feel any better, I feel the same way."

"That I'm nuts? That isn't a comfort."

Cheryl turned red. "No. I mean me. I don't know you well enough to wonder about that."

"After what I told you the other day, I wouldn't be surprised if you thought I was."

"People tell me a lot of strange stuff."

"I bet they do."

She liked the sound of his voice. The way it resonated in her ear. She wanted to keep talking to him. That's why she said, "Maybe I can do something to help you. I would be willing to check out the situation at least. I think the cards might be able to help."

"Tarot cards can cast out ghosts?"

"Not really. I don't know. I just wanted to try. It wouldn't hurt to try, right?"

"It definitely wouldn't hurt. I'd be grateful to you forever if you could get rid of this thing."

"Eternal gratitude is good enough. I won't charge you since I have no idea what I'm doing."

"I should pay you. It's how you make your living."

"I make my living reading tarot cards not casting out demons."

"Nobody said it was a demon."

"You said it was angry."

"Angry, not demonic. Don't even put that idea in my head."

"I'm not trying to."

"Listen to me," he said. "Just a few years ago I didn't believe in any of this stuff, and now I'm asking a psychic to cast a spirit out of my house. The world must be coming to an end."

"Not the whole world, just your world."

He snorted. "Thanks a lot."

Cheryl didn't mean to sound negative. "Don't worry. I'll figure out how to help you. You'll just have to make it through tonight."

"I think I can manage that."

"You'd better." If she could help, she would. Sometimes she only needed to pretend she could, and that would be enough. She figured that out when she first started reading tarot cards. She had no idea what she was doing, but people believed her. They wanted what she said to be true. They'd come to her months after a reading and tell her about how everything she'd predicted had happened. Even though sometimes she felt like they were making connections where there weren't any, she liked it.

Cheryl was not looking forward to whatever was

waiting for her at home. She had been so happy to get out of the house that morning. Throughout the day she kept thinking about the phone calls, the high-pitched childlike voice, the crackling sound. Each time she thought about it she got chills. How could she help Adam if she couldn't help herself?

She needed to be brave and figure out what was happening. She took a deep breath. "You can do this," she said to herself before walking through the front door of her apartment.

The telephone rested on the end table, black plastic with buttons covering its face. The blinking red light on its base let her know a message was waiting for her. She didn't want to check it.

She started to dial the number to check the messages, her finger hovering over the last digit. She took a deep breath before pressing it and holding the cool receiver to her ear.

She was so nervous that when the robotic female voice on the other end asked her to type in her passcode, she almost forgot it. After some thought, it came to her, and she punched it in.

"You have one new message," the automated voice said.

Even though having one new message was out of the ordinary on this phone, Cheryl felt relieved. Part of her had been expecting to have twenty, thirty, or even a hundred messages. She pressed the button to listen to the new message and an excited voice started to speak.

"Congratulations! You have been chosen to win an all-expenses-paid vacation," the voice said.

Cheryl's shoulders dropped with relief, and the tension rushed from her body like water. She was expecting the childlike voice asking for help. She knew she didn't win anything. The message was a way to get her to call the number back and sell her something, but getting the message alone was enough to make her feel like a winner. Her apartment was just the way she'd left it. It hadn't been ransacked by poltergeists or turned into a gate to another dimension while she was gone. She sat down on the sofa and Beau quickly made his way to her lap. She tried to convince herself what happened yesterday was a nightmare she'd confused with reality. She liked that idea, better than the alternative. All day she'd been trying to figure out what the phone calls meant, but the idea they didn't mean anything because they hadn't happened sat with her much better.

That was the solution to her problem. She held Beau against her chest as she stood. She'd have to put together something to eat before her shift started with the psychic hotline. Then she could start looking into how to help Adam. She liked the idea of that. Thinking about how to help someone else was much better than walking around being afraid for herself.

CHAPTER FIVE

CHERYL stood at the apartment door for a few moments before knocking. A bundle of dried sage rested in her bag along with her deck of tarot cards and a few crystals. She didn't know if any of them would work. In truth, she doubted they would but was willing to give anything a try.

Adam opened the door as soon as she knocked. His dark hair was disheveled. He wasn't wearing his glasses, and dark circles sat beneath his bloodshot eyes. He was wearing a white T-shirt with a dime-sized hole in the left shoulder and a pair of denim shorts. He looked so different than the man she'd seen at the coffee shop that she almost didn't recognize him. She was used to the clean-cut, put-together version.

"I'm so glad you're finally here," he said. "Come in." He stepped aside to let her into the room.

The frantic look in his eyes, the way they darted from side to side made her hesitate. Should she go into this man's apartment? He seemed desperate and even dangerous. "Maybe this was a bad idea," she said. She looked down the hallway, hoping to see someone else. Someone who could be a witness if she disappeared. "I mean ... you look like this isn't a good time for you." She looked at her wrist as if looking at the watch she wasn't wearing. "I forgot I have an appointment with a client soon. I'm a bit flighty at times and forget these things. You know how it is. Fortune tellers aren't exactly known for our ..." She stopped. He was standing there staring at her, his face collapsing as she spoke.

"I thought you were going to help me."

When he spoke, she got a glimpse of what he must have looked like as a boy. The sadness in his expression touched her. She couldn't run away. She looked at her wrist again. "I guess I have time."

"Why do you keep looking at your wrist?" he asked. "You aren't wearing a watch."

"It's a habit. Ignore it." She stepped through the door into what she assumed must have been the living room. It was hard to tell because it was such a mess. Boxes were stacked high in every corner. Piles of clothes rested on the sofa, and dirty dishes were strewn across the coffee table. There was a path on the floor through the piles of clothes and trash. "What happened in here?" She looked around at the mess in awe.

"I'm not sure how it got this way." He picked up a few shirts from the couch and stood, holding them in his hands looking around at the mess like he was seeing it for the first time too. Exasperated, he dropped the shirts back on the sofa. "I moved. Then my girlfriend broke up with me, and my mother got sick. I was taking care of her, and the apartment got neglected. On top of that, there are the ghosts. It's like I woke up one day and it looked like this. It feels too far gone to do anything about."

Cheryl shook her head. She couldn't believe what she was seeing. Food crusted on plates and cups with moldy liquid floating in them. This man who she'd thought of as attractive before suddenly didn't look that good. "How do you live like this?"

"I don't know." He sat on the couch on top of the pile of clothes. "I just do. The ghosts don't help things."

Cheryl was so shocked by the look of the apartment the ghost had completely slipped her mind. "Don't blame this on the ghost. Spirits don't do this."

He leaned forward resting his head in his hands, his back rounded with shame.

How could she not feel sorry for him? "I'm not judging. I'm just saying this is the kind of environment that attracts spirits. No wonder you're haunted."

"I was haunted before I was living in a dump. It started in my last house which was very clean. This place was clean once too, but once the haunting started up again, I let it go."

"That's putting it mildly." She covered her mouth with her hand. Why couldn't she just shut up sometimes? "You can clean it up. I'll help you get it together." Now she was volunteering to help him clean? She hated cleaning her own house!

"I must seem like a crazy person." He looked up at her.

"No." She thought for a moment. "Okay. Yes, you do. Honestly, I'm shocked by the state of things. I didn't expect this."

"You don't have to help me. I can find someone else."

The words stung. Even though she wasn't eager to help him in the beginning, she was committed now. "I said I would help you, and I will."

"Before I started reading tarot I didn't believe in ghosts or spirits or even god. My world was very concrete. It was centered on what I could see, touch, hear, and smell, but working in this business has exposed me to a lot of different ideas." Her eyes widened. "A lot of stories. The more I heard, the more I started to believe. There's more to the world than what we can see. I know that for sure. If you say there are spirits haunting you I'm inclined to believe you. There is something going on here. Whether I'll be able to figure out what's happening to you is yet to be determined, but I know something must have driven you to live like this. I'd like to get to the bottom of it." She stood firmly or as firmly as she could with one foot on the carpet and the other on a stack of magazines. She reached up and adjusted her ponytail.

"Thank you for believing me. The few people I have told never do unless I'm paying them."

"What have you had done so far?" She needed to get an idea, so she knew what not to waste their time with. She'd looked up everything she could about how to exorcise spirits on the internet before she went to bed. She was far from an expert. She hadn't let that stop her when she started reading tarot though and wasn't going to let it stop her now.

"Well ..." He started listing things off, but Cheryl found it hard to focus on what he was saying. Her eyes trained on the arched doorway that led into the kitchen. She was being drawn into that room.

"Tell me about the kitchen." She interrupted his list.

"The kitchen," he said, looking at the archway that led into it. "What can I say?" He paused and rubbed his eyes with his hand. "That's where it all started, in this place at least."

"What happened?"

"What hasn't happened? Every time I'm in there I feel like someone else is in there with me. Sometimes I swear I can hear it breathing next to me." He ran his hand through his hair. "Do ghosts breathe?"

"Probably not."

He nodded and thought for a moment. "Of course not, but that's what it's like. I'd be looking in the refrigerator and swear someone was leaning over my shoulder breathing in my ear. That probably sounds like a little thing, but it's not when it's happening. When I first moved into this place, I always felt like someone was in the room with me. It wasn't a concrete feeling, nothing I could put my finger on, but it was happening that's for sure. It was happening all the time. I was never alone in this apartment. From the moment I moved in it, whatever 'it' is, has been right here with me." He let out an exhausted laugh. "Usually that's supposed to be comforting, you know, you're never alone and all that."

Cheryl nodded. She'd been told that many times, but it was never true. She was alone plenty in her life. She never felt more alone than when she was still with Carl. Laying on the floor after he'd beaten her during a drunken outrage she would pray for help, but she always felt alone. No one was listening to her prayers. No one noticed her bruises.

Somehow, her dark glasses did such a good job at hiding her black eyes no one ever suspected anything. Sometimes Cheryl thought about the people she saw every day back then: the neighbor who lived on the other side of their bedroom wall who must've heard everything but never called the police, the man who sold jewelry on the corner who she talked to every day with the taste of blood in her mouth, the old woman whose groceries she'd help carry inside with her arms marked with bruises. Every day she read for so many clients and not a single person said anything. No one offered to help her. No one answered her prayers. She was all alone. She was so alone she felt like she might disappear. She wished she would. She almost made herself disappear. She'd held a sharp blade to her wrists too many times to count. She couldn't do it though. That wasn't an option. She needed to help herself. She needed to answer her own prayers. If she hadn't, she wouldn't have been here today. Now she needed to help Adam do the same thing for himself. The state of his apartment told her he was in more trouble than she'd initially thought. He was losing himself to this ghost, like she'd lost herself to Carl. She was going to be there to help pull him out.

"What are you thinking?" he asked.

"Nothing. Keep going. Tell me how it started."

"I didn't start here. It started in a house I rented." He told her the story about the haunting of the first house he lived in and how he left to move into someplace new. "At first, this apartment was great. It was new, so I figured I wouldn't have anything to worry about. I was wrong. After about a week it started again. I would be in the kitchen heating something up in the microwave, and I'd feel someone breathing in my ear. When I sat on the couch to watch the game, it felt like someone was sitting next to me. I was uncomfortable in my own place. That was it at first, a general feeling of not being alone. It was creepy, but I was adjusting. Eventually, I got used to it. I stopped freaking out and started spending more time at home. I even named it Louise, because it's like a funny old lady name. I was coming to terms with things until the other day when Louise made physical contact with me. I didn't think that was possible. Did you know that was possible?"

"It physically touched you?" Cheryl didn't know that was possible. She already felt like she was in over her head.

"Yeah. I was in the bathroom shaving when it nudged me. It happened twice. The second time it was a good hard shove. After that, I put on my clothes and went to work early. I couldn't be in this apartment alone anymore that morning." He looked at her as if begging her to believe him.

"I don't know what's possible," Cheryl admitted. "If you're telling me that that's what happened to you it must be possible."

"What can you do about it?"

Suddenly the sage and crystals Cheryl had brought with her in her purse felt ineffective and even childish. What could she tell him? "I don't know what to do? I was kind of hoping to show up and have some idea intuitively, but I feel a bit confused. I guess I didn't believe you before, but now I'm here it's different." She opened the purse on her lap and pulled out her deck of tarot cards. She didn't know what she could do with these to help but they were reliable, like an old friend. She knew how to use them. "I could start by giving a reading." She thought of the sage in her bag again and decided to mention it. "I brought some sage to smudge the house."

"I've already had someone do that for me. It didn't work, but I guess we could try again."

Cheryl didn't like how defeated he sounded. "If you've already had it done there's no use in doing it again. Let's just do the reading."

"Okay then."

The kitchen was still calling her. She wanted to go in there but didn't want to at the same time. Dread rose in her throat. "Can we do the reading in there?" She nodded toward the arched kitchen door.

He cleared the dirty plates from the table, adding them to the pile overflowing from the sink. Seated at the blonde pine kitchen table, she removed the cards from their velvet satchel and handed them to Adam. "Shuffle the deck."

He took the cards from her reluctantly and began shuffling. The cards slapped against each other as they intermingled.

"You thought about the question you wanted to ask the cards, right?"

He nodded.

Cheryl took the deck from him. She closed her eyes and took a few slow deep breaths, focusing on Adam and the apartment. She could feel the spirit. Dark energy swirled in the air all around them. She started laying out the cards in a Celtic cross spread, the one she always used, but after she laid out the first two cards, tension gripped her chest.

She swallowed hard and stopped.

"Is something wrong?" Adam asked.

She tried to inhale and couldn't, her lungs contracting when they should have been expanding. She closed her eyes and tried to push away the panic.

"Cheryl?"

She opened her eyes. A man and a woman stood in front of the table. They wore party clothes. A beaded gown was draped over the woman's narrow frame. The man was dressed in a tuxedo. A top hat balanced at a jaunty angle on his head. It was as if they were there, but not there, all at once. Cheryl wasn't prepared to see, or explain, anything like this to anyone else. She took hold of Adam's arm, her fingertips digging into his flesh. "Can you see that?" she asked, her voice barely a whisper.

"What?" Adam swiveled, looking around the room.

"There!" Cheryl pointed at the couple standing directly in front of the table. "They're right there!" Her heart pounded in her chest. "Can't you see them?" The chill in the air wrapped around her. She picked up the tarot cards she'd placed on the table and added them back to the deck. Her heart was a wild animal, clawing at her rib cage. She stood and left the kitchen swiftly. Stumbling on a pile of clothes her knee hit the ground hard. She ignored the pain and sprang to her feet. Collecting her purse from the couch, she started toward the door.

"Wait!" Adam called after her. "You saw it? You saw my ghost! There's more than one?"

Cheryl wasn't listening, she was walking to the door. She needed to get out of there, now.

"You can't just leave!" Adam called after her. "You're supposed to be helping me. You said you would try to get rid of them."

She opened the door. When she turned around to speak to him, she saw them again. Two of them hovering just inches from the floor in the kitchen doorway. They were ghosts, actual ghosts. "I can't do this. I thought I could help you, but it turns out I can't. You have to find someone else." She opened the door and stepped out into the hallway, which even though it was a smaller narrower space, felt open and free. She marched down the stairs. Adam called after her, but her mind was so busy she didn't register what he said. He was right. She should've been helping him, but this was beyond anything she'd ever imagined. Was she losing her mind? Was she seeing things? Was being in that house talking to him enough to make people delusional? She wasn't sure. She needed to go home. She needed to sort all of this out for herself before she could move forward.

He took the cards from her reluctantly and began shuffling. The cards slapped against each other as they intermingled.

"You thought about the question you wanted to ask the cards, right?"

He nodded.

Cheryl took the deck from him. She closed her eyes and took a few slow deep breaths, focusing on Adam and the apartment. She could feel the spirit. Dark energy swirled in the air all around them. She started laying out the cards in a Celtic cross spread, the one she always used, but after she laid out the first two cards, tension gripped her chest.

She swallowed hard and stopped.

"Is something wrong?" Adam asked.

She tried to inhale and couldn't, her lungs contracting when they should have been expanding. She closed her eyes and tried to push away the panic.

"Cheryl?"

She opened her eyes. A man and a woman stood in front of the table. They wore party clothes. A beaded gown was draped over the woman's narrow frame. The man was dressed in a tuxedo. A top hat balanced at a jaunty angle on his head. It was as if they were there, but not there, all at once. Cheryl wasn't prepared to see, or explain, anything like this to anyone else. She took hold of Adam's arm, her fingertips digging into his flesh. "Can you see that?" she asked, her voice barely a whisper.

"What?" Adam swiveled, looking around the room.

"There!" Cheryl pointed at the couple standing directly in front of the table. "They're right there!" Her heart pounded in her chest. "Can't you see them?" The chill in the air wrapped around her. She picked up the tarot cards she'd placed on the table and added them back to the deck. Her heart was a wild animal, clawing at her rib cage. She stood and left the kitchen swiftly. Stumbling on a pile of clothes her knee hit the ground hard. She ignored the pain and sprang to her feet. Collecting her purse from the couch, she started toward the door.

"Wait!" Adam called after her. "You saw it? You saw my ghost! There's more than one?"

Cheryl wasn't listening, she was walking to the door. She needed to get out of there, now.

"You can't just leave!" Adam called after her. "You're supposed to be helping me. You said you would try to get rid of them."

She opened the door. When she turned around to speak to him, she saw them again. Two of them hovering just inches from the floor in the kitchen doorway. They were ghosts, actual ghosts. "I can't do this. I thought I could help you, but it turns out I can't. You have to find someone else." She opened the door and stepped out into the hallway, which even though it was a smaller narrower space, felt open and free. She marched down the stairs. Adam called after her, but her mind was so busy she didn't register what he said. He was right. She should've been helping him, but this was beyond anything she'd ever imagined. Was she losing her mind? Was she seeing things? Was being in that house talking to him enough to make people delusional? She wasn't sure. She needed to go home. She needed to sort all of this out for herself before she could move forward.

CHAPTER SIX

THE bangles on her wrists clanked together as she ran down the steps away from him, her full skirt trailing behind her. Adam called after her. She didn't turn around to answer him. He had the right to be angry. She was running away just when she could've been the most help. Living with the ghosts every day had caused something to snap in him. He couldn't imagine what it must have been like for her, experiencing them for the first time.

She had seen them. There was more than one. He'd suspected all along but couldn't have been sure until now. He only felt them: brushing past him in the hall, an invisible hand on his shoulder, a shove in the kitchen, sometimes playful, sometimes angry, always unwanted. She had seen them. He wasn't crazy after all.

Once she disappeared down the stairwell, he went back into his condo and stood at the window looking out over the street where he could see her jogging up the block. She dropped her purse only a few yards from the door and had to stop. Stooping over, she shoved the contents inside before she took off again. She left something on the sidewalk. From that far up he couldn't make out what it was.

Adam slid on his sandals and went outside. He took the stairs just like she had and stepped out into the balmy weather. He saw what she had dropped immediately. There was no one on the street, so there was no one to take it. A dark blue stone, the size of a small plum, lay on the sidewalk. Flecked with gold, it glimmered in the sunlight. He looked around to see if he saw anything else. He wasn't sure if this was the thing she had dropped. There was no evidence of anything that should've been in the woman's purse, so he picked up the stone assuming it was hers. He would return it to her the next time he went to the coffee shop. He held it in his hand. He liked the feel of it in his palm. Feeling the warmth of the heat of the sun on his neck, he considered for a minute not going back inside. The sky hung clear and lovely overhead. Inside, uncertainty waited. He never knew when his roommates from the other side might decide to get frisky again, but he didn't have his keys or his wallet. He kept the stone in his hand because the weight of it reminded him of the shape of reality. He went back inside, walked over to the elevator, and pushed the button to go up. He was in no hurry.

Inside, the condo was cold and lonely. It was strange how having her there for only a few minutes made such a difference to him. She filled up the space, and until she told him she had seen them, he thought she had pushed the ghosts out completely.

He checked the thermostat. It was set to seventy-five

degrees as usual. Why did it feel so much colder? The spirits were still there with him. He couldn't sense them now, but he knew they were lingering, waiting to make themselves known again. Often, he could feel them around him, hovering, looking over his shoulder like they were trying to tell him something. He put the blue stone down on the coffee table and started looking for his wallet. It wasn't on the cabinet by the door. He thought he could remember putting it there the previous night. He always did. He found himself wondering if the ghosts had moved it but dismissed that thought as quickly as he had it. He talked to them as he walked from room to room in his apartment looking for his wallet. "I don't like it when you move my things," he said.

He found his wallet in the bathroom, balanced on the edge of the sink. He knew he hadn't put it there. He collected it and his keys, put on a better pair of shoes, and headed out of the house. He couldn't stay there any longer, not today. He'd have to find someplace else to spend his day. It was Saturday, and there was always a ton of stuff to do in the city. Unfortunately, the ghosts would still be there when he got back home.

He'd had all kinds of people who claimed psychic abilities over to his place to exorcise the spirits haunting him. Some claimed to sense them, but no one ever saw them, not as clearly as Cheryl had.

A woman who smelled of incense and laundry detergent waved a bundle of burning sage while reciting a prayer in a language Adam couldn't understand. When she'd finished, she'd told him the ghosts were gone. They weren't. A man walked around his house holding a stick that would spin in his hand when he got near a ghost. His stick spun five times while he was in Adam's apartment and every time Adam could see the ropy muscles in his forearm flex. He'd had aura readers, witches, and mystics wander around his living space leaving small bundles of herbs and candles with him to scare off the spirits. The funny part was before all of this started he didn't believe in any of this. He never thought he would hire these types of people. He still didn't believe. Not until Cheryl showed up. She was the real deal, and if anyone could help him, she could. He only needed to convince her to come back. He wouldn't do that now. Judging by the way she ran out the door she needed time to process what she'd seen. She'd be back though. He knew it.

He usually liked to look a little better when he went out, but he wasn't eager to spend time in the apartment, so he didn't change his torn T-shirt or ratty shorts. He'd worn the T-shirt that day because it was lucky, and he thought he needed all the luck he could get. He slipped the stone into his pocket because he felt like it grounded him. When he stepped back out into the hallway, the lightness of the air was a relief. His apartment had a heaviness that drained him. The Saturday morning market was going on, and he knew he could go there to get something to eat and maybe even bump into some friends.

"Hey, Adam!" a voice yelled at him as he attempted to squeeze through the crowd in front of the Thai food booth.

The market was teeming with people. Adam hadn't

been to it in more than a month and didn't remember it ever being this busy. He craned his neck and saw a hand waving at him over the crowd. "Excuse me. Pardon me. Sorry." He worked his way through the crush of people and came out on the other end to an open space on the blacktop. "Mitchell," he said upon seeing the stalky man in shorts in a Hawaiian shirt standing before him.

Adam worked with Mitchell years ago. "It's been forever." Mitchell gave him a combination handshake hug that made Adam feel a bit uncomfortable.

"How have you been?" A group of people jostled him as they passed.

"I've had the craziest year." Mitchell's voice boomed over the jangly guitar sounds of the band playing a few yards from them.

"Really? What's been going on?" He was sure whatever Mitchell said would be nothing compared to what he was experiencing.

Mitchell ran a hand through his spiky blond hair and started to smile. "I got married. It was fast, but when you know, you know."

"Oh, okay. Congratulations." This wasn't what Adam was expecting to hear. Because of his own problems he'd assumed Mitchell was about to deliver bad news.

"I knew as soon as I met her, but I waited a few months before I asked. I didn't want to seem insane." He let out a laugh. "We bought a house this year, and I got a promotion."

"That's great, man."

"I know. It's like when good stuff happens it keeps

happening. I'm trying to remember to appreciate it because who knows when the rug will get pulled out from under me." A laugh erupted from his belly, and he hit Adam in the arm a little too hard. "The other shoe has to drop sometime."

"It has for me."

Mitchell frowned. "I'm sorry. And here I am bragging about my good fortune. What's going on with you?"

Adam shrugged. "It's too hard to explain. Let's just say I'm stressed these days."

Mitchell shook his head. "You ought to start doing tai chi or something. I started doing it a few months ago. It's great." He stepped into a wide stance and started moving his hands slowly like he was balancing a cup in his palm.

"I'll try that." Adam was willing to try anything that would get him out of the house. "I think you're right. My luck is bound to change soon."

"What goes up must come down." He scratched his face. "I mean the other way around."

"It wouldn't make sense the other way around, but I know what you mean." After talking to Mitchell, Adam looked around the market a bit more. He kept thinking about what Mitchell had said. Ever since this haunting began, he kept wondering what he would do if these ghosts harassed him for the rest of his life? It couldn't stay this bad forever.

There was Cheryl. She was his light at the end of the tunnel, not just because she'd seen the ghosts, but because the rhythm of her voice could make him forget how difficult it had become for him at home. He saw hope in her cinnamon eyes. He reached into his pocket and felt the reassuring weight of the blue stone she'd dropped on the sidewalk. This wouldn't last forever because Adam wouldn't let it, and he had Cheryl to help him get rid of these ghosts, once and for all.

CHAPTER SEVEN

CHERYL splashed cold water on her face. She felt like she was going to pass out and had honestly considered going to the hospital instead of going home. She thought maybe she'd had a seizure or a stroke. She'd heard once that sometimes, when people have a stroke, they see things that aren't there. Was she just moments away from death? After thinking about it for a good long time, she decided against going to the hospital. She didn't want to end up in the psych ward. She wasn't prepared for that. She'd seen One Flew Over the Cuckoo's Nest and Girl Interrupted.

She filled her cupped hands with more ice-cold water and splashed it on her face. The sting of the cold water reminded her she was alive. She looked at herself in the mirror. Droplets of water hung from her nose and her chin. She half expected to see someone standing behind her. Since when had her life turned into a cheap horror movie?

She grabbed the white towel hanging on the rack next to the sink and dried her face not caring if she smeared it with makeup. Her cell phone started to ring in the next room, and for a minute she considered not answering it. After it rang for a while, she changed her mind and hurried into the living room to find it in her purse.

"Hello?"

"You'll never guess what happened to me," the voice on the other end said. It was her friend Stephanie.

"You'll never guess what happened to me," Cheryl said back to her.

"I'm intrigued, but I want to go first." Stephanie and Cheryl had met in a yoga class years ago. It was both of their first time taking hot yoga, and after sweating buckets for an hour and a half, it was their last. In the parking lot after class, they joked with each other about how terrible it was and how they didn't understand all the people claiming to feel great afterward in the lobby. Cheryl had spent the whole class trying desperately not to faint or vomit or both. She thought it was just her, but when she saw Stephanie red-faced and panting in the parking lot, she guessed she might've felt the same way.

"I'm never coming back to this class," Cheryl had said to Stephanie over the roofs of the parked cars. When Stephanie agreed, she knew it was safe to lay into how terrible the class had been for her. Being dehydrated and twisted into impossible positions for that long was enough to give anyone a headache. They'd become fast friends. Cheryl was new in town back then, and she needed a friend. Even though they didn't see each other as much as they wanted anymore, they made time to speak on the phone. Talking on the phone was important to Stephanie who wasn't fond of all the texting people did these days. Cheryl liked their phone calls too. Stephanie seemed to have a special sense that let her know the exact right time to call, like now.

"Remember how I told you about my neighbor?" Stephanie said into the phone.

"You mean the one you're always telling me is so hot." Cheryl raised her voice trying to mimic Stephanie's.

Stephanie laughed. "There are several of those, but this one is the artist."

"Yeah, I remember." Stephanie had talked about that particular neighbor more than the others.

"He's been depressed recently. His girlfriend dumped him, so I've been trying to cheer him up by bringing by takeout, and inviting him out with me, and stuff like that. Anyway, we're going out. It's only been a few times, but he seems like he's interested all of a sudden."

Stephanie was the flirtatious type who had no problem finding a boyfriend. There'd been many since she and Cheryl had been friends. Cheryl, on the other hand, managed to stay single. She liked it that way. Her last relationship made her afraid to get too involved with anyone. She didn't want to end up in that situation again. "Don't get too excited. He's on the rebound."

"They were together hardly any time at all. I don't think it's that much of a rebound and I've been feeling like I'm ready to settle down. He seems like the settling down type. Everybody I know is getting married and having kids."

"I'm not."

"You'd need to go out on a few dates first." She was always trying to set Cheryl up with guys she worked with, but Cheryl always refused. "I know I'm jumping the gun a little, but I'm pretty excited. I'm trying to keep things realistic and tamp down my feelings a bit, but I just had to tell somebody."

"Congratulations. I hope it works out," Cheryl said, wondering how long this would last. Stephanie tended to tire of her boyfriends quickly.

"I think this one will," Stephanie said. "So, what's your news?"

Cheryl cleared her throat. She felt like she could tell Stephanie anything, but this was the first time she'd told anyone she saw a ghost. "I went to see a client this morning. He said he was being haunted and even though that's not something I normally do I decided to see if I could help. I went over there, and the apartment was a mess, clothes, dishes, and boxes everywhere."

"A hoarder."

"I don't think so. He said that he didn't like being in the place since the ghosts showed up, so he stopped cleaning."

Stephanie laughed. "That's why I stopped washing the dishes. I can't deal with the ghost living in my sink."

"I saw a ghost in his kitchen—two ghosts."

"You did not."

"I swear on my own life." Cheryl was used to swearing on her life. She always said that when she was trying to prove she was telling the truth. "After I saw them I bolted."

Stephanie laughed. "I'm sure you did. I like to pretend I'm brave, but I probably would've done the same thing."

Cheryl laughed. "You definitely would've done the same thing. Don't even pretend." She bit her lip. "Now I keep wondering whether I saw ghosts or not. It all could've been a figment of my imagination. Maybe I'm going crazy."

"Join the club," Stephanie said.

"Very funny. I'm serious. I got some weird phone calls yesterday."

"What phone calls?"

"They came through on the landline. Nobody has that number. It only rings for my work with the hotline. Anyway, it was just a crackling sound like the line was bad, and then underneath I could hear a creepy kid's voice asking for help. It freaked me out. Then this happens today. I'm questioning my sanity that's all."

Stephanie laughed. "That's all?"

Cheryl did see the humor in it, but she was too nervous to laugh. "What should I do?"

"I think you need to commit yourself to a mental hospital."

Her voice was so somber when she said it that Cheryl was silently considering doing it.

"I'm joking," Stephanie said. "You didn't take me seriously, did you?"

Cheryl swallowed. "Of course not."

"Just wait and see if anything happens again. If it does, call me right away."

"Because you're good at protecting people from

ghosts?"

"I was a ghostbuster this past Halloween." She let out a belly laugh. "A sexy ghostbuster."

"I don't even want to know." Cheryl paused for a moment. "When I went to this guy's place I was kind of thinking he might be crazy. I've seen him at the coffee shop a lot, but I never talked to him. When he told me why he wanted me to come to his place I thought he might have a few screws loose."

"If you thought that, you shouldn't have gone. I shouldn't have to tell you that."

Cheryl had thought of that when she left to go to Adam's house that morning. She considered calling Stephanie and telling her exactly where she would be, so she would know if something had happened to her. "I know, but that's not the point."

"It's important. Promise you'll do it next time. Send me a text and give me the address of the place. You never know with people these days."

Stephanie tended to be protective of her, and Cheryl appreciated that because her own family never seemed to care as much. She moved miles away and she hardly ever heard from them. "I will. Can I get on with my story now?"

"Of course."

"I went to his house and it was kind of weird. While he was telling me about the ghost, I kept having this strange feeling like someone was in the kitchen. I needed to go into the kitchen. I told him I was going to do a reading at his kitchen table, but I got this feeling that was...

I don't know how to describe it. It was almost like the nervousness you feel before you're getting on a stage in front of tons of people."

"That doesn't make me nervous at all," Stephanie said.

Cheryl was so eager to finish the story she ignored Stephanie's comment. "Anyway, I had this nervous tingling feeling in my stomach and chest as I started laying out the cards. When I looked up, I saw two people standing behind him. They weren't supposed to be there. I mean it was just the two of us in the apartment, him and me. There was no one else, but there were two people standing behind him dressed in old-fashioned clothes like they were in the Great Gatsby movie or something." Cheryl was starting to get a tingling feeling in her stomach and her chest just talking about it. She closed her eyes, and she could picture the man and the woman in her mind.

"Creepy. Tell me more."

"Don't act like this is some made up ghost story kids tell around the campfire at night. This is what happened to me." Stephanie loved a good horror movie. She read Stephen King books like they were going out of style. Cheryl never understood the desire to be scared.

"I know. I want to hear what happened next. Obviously, the ghosts didn't get you because you're still here."

"The ghosts didn't get me because I packed up my cards and ran out of there like somebody was chasing me. Somebody could've been. For all I know, I brought the ghosts back with me here." A chill went down her spine thinking of the phone call she'd received the day before. She looked over at the landline, a sleeping monster in her living room.

"You are too much, Cheryl. Seriously, if anything strange starts happening at your place, call me. You can sleep over here. You know I'd love the company."

"Thanks."

"I've got to go," Stephanie said. "I just wanted to tell you my news."

"Okay. I'll call you if I need you."

Talking to Stephanie always made Cheryl feel better. Stephanie was so light-hearted and fun. Cheryl appreciated that. She needed someone to remind her to take life less seriously. She'd become the closest thing to family she had in town. Her own family back in Minneapolis wasn't very dependable. Most of the time Cheryl felt like she was an orphan. She hadn't spoken to her mother or her brothers in so many years she had no idea what they were doing now. That was partially her fault. She was just as guilty of not calling them as they were of not calling her.

She sat back on the sofa and tried to relax. When she closed her eyes, she could see them again, two figures standing in the kitchen in front of Adam's sink. Their willowy limbs and slightly transparent bodies sent icicles through her heart. She opened her eyes again half expecting to see them standing in front of her. They weren't. Beau jumped up on the sofa next to her. He yawned before curling his body on the sofa cushion and closing his amber eyes to sleep.

Cheryl's living room, with tapestries on the walls and the worn floral sofa, didn't quite feel like hers anymore. The telephone sitting on the end table was like a time bomb. Each time she looked at it she expected it to go off. She checked the time. She'd have to log on to take calls in an hour. That gave her enough time to do some research.

Even though Cheryl worked as a fortuneteller, she always assumed most of the cases of ghosts she heard about weren't real, but her sense of what was real and what was not was shifting. It made her feel like the ground beneath her feet was crumbling. She had seen something. She didn't know why but she had seen something. She didn't think she was crazy, and if she wasn't crazy, there was only one other alternative.

Her cell phone rang. She picked it up and looked at the screen. It was Adam. She hit the red phone icon to ignore the call and continue typing on her computer. Her cell phone vibrated on the table letting her know he left a message. She would listen to it later.

Cheryl had a client once who told her that her house was haunted. She had actually had quite a few clients tell her that, but one client stood out. The narrow woman with nicotine-stained fingers and sour breath. She'd opened the reading with the story of her haunting saying, "I need to know how I can help the ghost that lives in my house." The question took Cheryl by surprise because she was so used to people wanting readings to find out about themselves. Occasionally people would ask about someone else in their lives, but no one had ever asked about a ghost. Noticing the surprise in Cheryl's eyes the woman elaborated. "He wakes me up every night. I know he needs something, but I can't figure out what."

That was one of those readings that Cheryl wasn't sure if she got right. She was so dependent on observing the person's body language and asking questions to make sure she gave them an appropriate reading. They always gave her clues, but this reading was cold because she could not observe a ghost. Instead, she gave a reading based on the woman and the mental disease Cheryl thought the woman might have. The woman recognized that almost immediately. A few cards into the reading she slammed her palm down on the table. "I need you to read for him, not me." Her brow furrowed with frustration.

There were only a few instances when Cheryl wished a reading was over. Usually, she enjoyed it because she felt like she was helping. When she wasn't helping she wanted it to end and this was one of those times. She'd looked up at the woman. "I'm sorry, but if I don't know about you how am I supposed to know about the being haunting you." She stayed calm. Cheryl's flustered demeanor made her seem like she'd crumble when even an ounce of pressure was put on her, but that was far from the truth. When she was working with her clients, she was a model of professionalism, except for that morning with Adam when she lost her cool completely. She sighed. She didn't want to have to work with him again, but there was no getting around it. She closed her computer. She didn't know what she was looking for anyway. She could only hope her upcoming shift on the Spirit Guides Hotline would help her think of what to do. Sometimes she got ideas for her own life when she did a reading. It didn't always happen, but she needed it to happen today. She sat on her couch awake but doing nothing and waited for her shift to start. She'd have to do something about Adam and his ghosts eventually. She couldn't put it off forever.

Chapter Eight

IT was eleven in the morning when Cheryl opened the door to the Starlight Café and walked in. She wasn't surprised to see Adam sitting at the bar drinking a cappuccino. He didn't have his laptop.

Cheryl had barely gotten in the door when he got up from his stool and walked over to her. She raised her hand telling him to stop, but he ignored her. Pressing into her space, he said, "I need you to come back to my place."

Cheryl walked past him to the back of the café where she normally did her readings. "I can't do this now. I have to work." She set her bag on the table and started rummaging through it.

"Okay. I need a reading." Adam pulled his wallet from his pocket and put it on the table before sitting down.

"I don't want to give you a reading. I want to work with real clients. I can't do anything to help you right now. I've already told you that." She took her deck of tarot cards out of her purse and put them on the table. "If you sit here, people are going to think I'm busy. I need as many clients as I can get, Adam. I have to pay my bills and things have been kind of slow recently."

"That's why I'm paying you to give me a reading." He picked his wallet up from the table and opened it.

Cheryl looked around at the other customers in the café. She felt like he was making a scene, but no one else seemed to notice. They were all engaged in their conversations, sucked into their screens, reading books, none of them seemed to notice anything Cheryl and Adam were doing. "If you want a reading, I'll give you a reading, but that's it. I'm not going to talk about what happened the other day."

"I thought you wanted to help me."

"I do, but I don't know how yet. I need time to think about it." She settled into the chair next to him. "Honestly, I was hoping you wouldn't be here today."

"Gee, thanks for the honesty." His voice dripped with sarcasm.

"Let me finish. I was hoping you wouldn't be here because I didn't know what to tell you yet. I want to help you. I really do. It's just what I saw the other day freaked me out. I've been going through a lot of stuff right now ..." Her ears rang with that crackling sound every time she thought about the phone calls. "... weird stuff. Mixing that all up with what happened at your place has been a bit much for me. It's like all this time I thought the world was one way and it wasn't. My idea of what is real and what isn't is out of whack. It's hard to recover from that." She threw her hands up in the air. "I don't know what I'm supposed to do. This is all fine for you because it's been going on for a while, but this is the first time I've heard anything about it. I've been living in this world where everything is concrete. I can see what's around me, and it's all explainable. Suddenly it's not anymore. It's not just what happened at your house. It's the things I can't talk about in my house too. It's throwing my whole sense of reality out of whack. What am I supposed to do? How am I supposed to deal with this?" She stared at him for a few minutes blinking. She needed answers. Answers would help everything and even though she knew he probably had none to give it was worth asking, waiting to see.

He waited a little too long to answer her. "I don't know. I'm still trying to figure all this out myself. My world's been turned upside down too. Sure, it's been a bit longer than you, but it's not like I'm used to it."

She cocked her head at him.

"Okay a lot longer than you, but I don't know what to do about it either. That's why I came to you. I was looking for answers."

Cheryl was the one who presented herself as an expert in the unseen world. Now she had seen the unseen, the fact she wasn't an expert at all was coming to light. She needed help, a way to make life normal again. "Fair enough. I don't have any answers though."

A dark-haired woman in a sundress wandered over to Cheryl's table and stood looking at her sign. "Excuse me," the woman said. "Do I need to make an appointment for a reading?"

Cheryl stood. "No, not at all. In fact, I can give you a reading right now." She glared at Adam.

"I was just leaving." He picked his wallet up from the table and stood. Before walking away, he pulled the blue stone from his pocket. "You dropped this the other day."

She knew the stone well, the constellation of golden dots like stars, that particular shade of deep blue. It was lucky. She'd found it in high school by a river bed in the woods behind her house. It was unlike any of the other rocks in the river, smooth grays and blacks. She'd fished it from the water, the cold stinging her fingers, the edge of her sleeve dunked into the icy current. The stone was lucky. She knew it. How could something so beautiful not be? She'd needed luck more than anything at the time. Cheryl carried that rock with her every day since she'd found it. She reached out and took it from him. "Thank you," she said. "It's important to me."

"It must not be that important since you didn't notice it was gone."

She scowled. "I've been going through a lot. I already told you that."

"I can come back for a reading some other time," the woman said, shifting her weight from one foot to the other.

"He's leaving." Cheryl widened her eyes at Adam.

"I'm going. Thanks so much for the reading," he said. "What you said is right on the money." He looked at the woman. "She's good. I swear, a reading from her will change your life." He turned back to Cheryl and winked.

Cheryl glanced nervously at the waiting woman. Adam's wink wasn't subtle. "Have a seat." Cheryl pulled the chair out from the table.

"I'll see you later," Adam said before leaving the coffee

shop.

It was a slow day for Cheryl. She only did that one reading and even though the coffee shop was crowded all day no one came over to her table. Frustrated, she decided to pack up early. Before leaving she went over to the counter to ask the barista to make her a latte. It was the same one as before with a short blonde pixie cut and nose ring. When Cheryl ordered, the barista looked around nervously before finally saying, "Connie wants to talk to you. I'm going to go get her." She went into the back room, leaving Cheryl standing at the counter.

Connie came bounding through in khaki slacks and a powder-blue polo shirt. Her full cheeks were flushed. Her usual smile was replaced by a much more serious expression. She walked out from around the counter and right up to Cheryl.

"It's been a long time," Cheryl said. She could tell from Connie's expression this wasn't going to be a good talk.

"It has." Connie glanced around the café. The crowd was beginning to thin. "Let's sit in the back. I need to talk to you for a minute."

"Is something wrong?" Cheryl asked.

Connie's stride was purposeful as she made a beeline to the table in the back corner of the café. "Have a seat." Connie pulled out a chair.

Cheryl sat down. As soon as her butt hit the chair, she started to talk. "I've been doing a lot of readings. Today was slow, but most days it's good. I think the customers like it. I have a lot of return people. Even if they come in specifically for a reading, they always buy a drink. Some people stay long after the reading to have pastries and more coffee. It's working out well, don't you think?"

"The baristas have told me you said part of our deal was you get free espresso drinks. Is that right?"

Cheryl shifted in her chair and cleared her throat. "When we made this arrangement, I thought that was part of the deal."

Connie crossed her arms and leaned back in her chair. "That would be an interesting deal for me to make considering I'm letting you do readings here for free. So, giving you free espresso drinks would be like I was paying you to use my space to run your business. Would that make sense?"

"Yes. I mean, no. I guess it doesn't make much sense."

"Originally, when we made this deal you were supposed to give me twenty percent of your earnings here. Do you remember that part of the deal?"

Cheryl tensed. "I thought when I explained to you how tight money has been for me recently, you said I didn't have to pay you. That's what I remember. Am I wrong?" They had never made formal arrangements for any of this. Cheryl watched Connie who sat with her arms crossed staring at her. "I'm probably wrong. I mishear things all the time. I think it's because I do more talking than listening most of the time. You're right, it doesn't make any sense for you to let me work here for free. You are an excellent businesswoman, and no one in business would agree to that kind of deal." Connie's silence scared Cheryl. Her throat suddenly felt parched. She cleared it and continued to talk. "I could pay you now if that's what you want." She pulled her wallet from her purse. Looking through it she saw that she had a few receipts and four dollars. "I don't have any cash to give you now."

"Would you even know how much to give me off hand?"

Cheryl sighed. She was terrible at keeping track of her finances. She had no idea how many people she'd read for at the café until now, but she figured she could estimate. She'd be sure to round up whatever number she came up with so Connie would get a reasonable amount of money. "No, but I'll figure it out tonight."

"This is disappointing. I was willing to trust you."

"I know," Cheryl said. "I appreciate this opportunity. It's been a lifesaver. I was thinking I could pay you the money all in one lump sum tomorrow."

"How long have you been reading here? Three months now? In a situation like this, you should be paying me monthly. This is partly my fault. I didn't approach this like a real business deal. There's no contract or anything. That was a mistake. I'm willing to admit that. I don't usually do business like that, but you seemed honest, and you do good work."

"I am honest," Cheryl said.

Connie knit her brow. "I was hoping I wouldn't have to chase you up for money and you wouldn't be stealing espresso drinks from me." Connie's face was tight. Everything about her posture was tight, her crossed arms and legs, the way she seemed to press herself into the chair.

"I'm sorry. I was wrong. I don't know what I was thinking. I'm just so unorganized. I love doing readings here. I have some regular people come back. They really like me. The vibe here is chill. Starlight is such a nice place. I think having a tarot card reader fits in with the image you're trying to project." Cheryl knew, no matter how much she talked or how many compliments she gave, she was about to get fired. Technically she wasn't fired because technically she wasn't working for Connie, but she knew everything was about to go sideways.

Connie just sat there looking at her with her arms crossed and her lips pursed.

"I really need this. It helps me make some extra money. I'm barely scraping by as it is." She didn't mean to go into groveling mode so soon. "The espresso drinks thing was a mistake. I'll pay for any coffee I get from now on if you just let me keep doing readings here."

Connie looked over to the counter watching the barista for a few moments then back at Cheryl. "This place gets pretty busy in the afternoons and having you taking up a table isn't in the best interest of the business. I thought this was going to work out, Cheryl, but it isn't. I'm sorry, but I don't want you to do readings here anymore."

"I can pay you the money I owe you. It's only a little over three hundred dollars." She pulled that figure out of thin air. She didn't even think she had that much money in the bank at the moment. If she asked, Stephanie would probably loan it to her though. "I don't have it now, but I can bring it to you tomorrow."

"Don't worry about it." Connie stood. "I'd prefer it if

we just went our separate ways."

Cheryl was too stunned to say anything else.

"I hope there's no hard feelings between us. This is a business decision for me. Don't take it personally." Connie stood and looked at her like she was expecting Cheryl to say something.

Cheryl bit her lip. She thought about her empty bank account. "No hard feelings," she said. "I guess I understand. You have to do what's best for the café."

Connie stuck out her hand, and Cheryl shook it. She left the café without saying goodbye to anyone. She'd planned on going home and looking into what she needed to do to help Adam, but now she was too caught up in what had just happened to even think about ghosts. Her self-pity party didn't last long. As she pushed open her apartment door, the landline was ringing. The shrill bell cut through the air. She stood in the entryway with her heart pounding in her chest, the bell slicing the air, piercing her eardrums. It rang again and again. She was frozen, wondering when it would stop. When it did, silence hung heavy in the air, almost tangible enough to hold. She walked over to the phone leaving the apartment door open behind her. She picked up the receiver and listened to the dial tone. The intermittent tone told her she had a new voicemail. She'd listen to it later. She'd do everything later. Now she needed time with a carton of ice cream and some television to clear her head. There was too much happening in her life to process. She needed time.

Chapter Nine

ADAM couldn't stay out forever. He walked through the house to the kitchen and lowered himself into the hard, wooden chair. "I'm back," he said. "In case you missed me." He listened, half expecting to hear someone. "If you tell me what you want I could help you out. Then you could move on and give me a break," he said into the empty air. He knew getting rid of his ghosts wasn't that simple. If it was, he would've been rid of them ages ago, but he wasn't one to give up hope. If he had given up easily, he wouldn't have gotten as far as he had in life. The refrigerator clicked on. It rattled so loudly he could hardly hear himself think. "I'm waiting." He looked around. "Where are you?"

Adam liked ghost stories as a kid. He would sit in the dark basement with his friends holding flashlights to their faces as they relayed terrifying tales to each other. Then he looked forward to the knot of fear in his stomach with gleeful anticipation.

"You're not talking today?" He strained to listen to nothing. "Maybe you're shy. I'll leave this here." He pointed at his phone. "If you have something to say, say it into here. I'm going to take a shower." He opened the voice recorder app on his cell phone and hit record before going to the bathroom.

The bathroom filled with steam as Adam let the hot water run over him. When the ghost first appeared in his life, he couldn't bear to take a shower. He wanted to be able to hear everything. He'd hardly slept. He'd go to work with bloodshot eyes, his thoughts like wading through molasses. Back then, he only showered in the gym because at least he knew the ghosts weren't there. Ghosts ... It was all so unbelievable to him. He understood why people didn't believe him. He wouldn't have either until it happened to him. Didn't hauntings only happen to people with small children who could be possessed? That was what he saw in the movies. The demon would enter the body of an already creepy-looking child and make her throw up black goo and spin her head all the way around. That was what hauntings were, but somehow his ghosts hadn't gotten that memo. No ghost had found their way into him, not that he had known at least. They found their way into his home and his life, but his body remained his own.

Even now, taking a shower made him feel a little ill at ease. When he turned off the water, he listened as the last of it rushed down the pipe. The plastic rings clacked together as he pushed the shower curtain open. He stood in the tub for a few moments listening to the whir of the bathroom fan. Then took a deep breath before pulling a towel from the rack and beginning to dry himself.

He stepped out of the tub with the towel draped over

his head, drying his short dark brown hair vigorously. The bathmat was soft beneath his feet. Pulling the towel from his head, he looked over at the bathroom mirror to see a word written in the condensation. The soft cursive of the looping letters was a stark contrast to the heaviness he felt in his chest.

"Sorry."

Icy coldness spread across his body from his stomach, creeping down him like a frost. He swallowed hard, his throat small and tight, his breathing ragged. He wrapped the towel around his waist. Droplets of water clung to his legs

"Sorry? Sorry for what?" Frustration pulsed through him. "If you're so sorry, why don't you stop?"

The bathroom door slammed shut. He took hold of the knob and yanked it open as hard as he could. He was expecting resistance, but there was none. The door flung open hitting his foot. He yelped with pain. He went to the bedroom and grabbed some clean clothes to put on. He needed to get out the house. He had no idea where he was going. He put on a pair of flip-flops before going into the kitchen and retrieving his phone from the table. He stopped the voice recorder and rushed toward the door. The phone started to vibrate in his hand. He looked at the screen. It was his sister, Julia. "Hey, Jules. What's going on?" He checked for his wallet before stepping out of the door and locking it.

"Nothing. I suddenly felt like I should call you. Are you all right?"

It was good to hear the familiar voice of someone he could trust. His sister, Julia, was six years older than him and had always been more like a mother than sister. Their own mother was too sick to parent them properly. It was Julia who signed permission slips, packed school lunches, and fixed dinner each night. Adam took a few deep breaths and started down the stairs. "Everything's good."

"You can't lie to me, little brother. I practically raised you."

Adam had told her about the ghost before, and when he did, she shook her head and kept suggesting he start seeing someone. He knew what that meant. Their mother saw and heard things no one else did. Sometimes she ripped her hair out with fear. Adam remembered sitting on the floor sucking on his two fingers, his stomach crying out for food as he watched his mother draw hundreds of circles in a notebook. She counted them aloud as she drew. When each page was full, she would tear it out, ball it up, and throw it to the floor. Stiff white snowballs covered the carpet. When he first noticed these ghosts, he thought about his mother. He wondered if he had what she had. That kind of sickness can be passed down to children, but he had felt saner than most until that day. He understood what it meant when Jules told him he should see somebody. He knew what she was thinking. He could see it in her eyes when they were together. "What are you doing tonight?" he asked her.

"We were going to see a movie, but our babysitter canceled. She has the flu." Adam's niece and nephew were four and six. He didn't spend as much time with them as he should, but he loved seeing their bright little faces. "How about I come over and sit for you? That way you guys can still have your date night, and I can see the little monsters."

"You're not busy?"

"I always have time for the little monsters; you know that. I'm upset you didn't call me to babysit in the first place." Adam was already out on the street walking to his car. "I'll be right over."

"That would be great, Adam. The kids will love to see you, but you have to follow the rules. They have to go to bed on time otherwise they're super cranky the next day."

"I always follow the rules." That was a lie, and Adam knew it. The last time he babysat for his niece and nephew he let them stay up almost two hours past their bedtime, so they could watch a movie on television. He told them that was fine as long as they didn't tell their mother. They weren't very good at keeping secrets.

"Thank you. I'll see you soon. I have to go so I can get ready." She hung up the phone.

Relief washed over him. He would have an excuse to be out of the house and not have to explain anything to Jules. Maybe he'd even come up with a reason to spend the night.

"Uncle Adam!" Chloe clung to the legs of his jeans. Adam pulled at his waistband afraid she might pull down his pants. He reached down and picked her up, carrying her under his arm. She giggled with delight as she kicked her legs. "I told Carson you're coming, but he didn't believe me," she said between fits of laughter.

Carson stood in the open doorway gnawing on a carrot

93

stick. "You're better than the babysitter." Carson beamed. He rocketed into the house. "Uncle Adam's here!"

Adam stepped into the cozy wooden bungalow as his sister came out of the hallway into the living room. She was putting an earring on. "I can't even begin to tell you how grateful I am."

"You're doing me a favor. I get to spend the night with the best kids in the world." He lowered Chloe to the floor, and she started running circles around him.

"Chloe, calm down." Jules reached out and caught her arm as she tried to run past her. "You'll be on your best behavior tonight, right?"

Chloe tried to wriggle away but was unsuccessful.

"You better behave yourself, missy." Jules was not letting go.

Defeated, Chloe stopped moving. She looked up at her mother and said, "I always behave." Jules and Carson started to laugh.

Chloe struggled with attention deficit disorder and hyperactivity. She was constantly in trouble at school before Jules decided to pull her out and start homeschooling her. She could get tiring, but Adam was pretty good at managing her. She was a little bit different, but different was good. And there were a lot of things she did that reminded him of himself when he was younger.

Carson was almost the exact opposite of Chloe. Shy and reserved, he stuck by his mother's side and always did what he was told.

Tim walked into the room. "You're a lifesaver," he said to Adam.

"Just let me know anytime I can save the day." Adam gave his brother-in-law a hug.

Jules called some instructions at him as they left the house. Adam stood with the children and watched them back out of the driveway. When the car was finally heading up the street, Chloe threw up her hands and said, "Let's have fun!"

Adam laughed. She was on fire tonight and would probably wear him out, but that was all right. They would help him forget what was waiting at his apartment.

It was getting late. Adam put the children to bed, and after reading five stories, Chloe had finally drifted off to sleep, her eyelids finding it hard to resist the call of dreams. Adam went out to the living room, sat down on the sofa, and turned on the television. The news was on. His thoughts drifted as the anchorwoman spoke to the camera. She was talking about a house fire and how the people inside escaped by jumping out the windows when he remembered he had pressed record on the voice recorder before getting in the shower. He picked the phone up off the coffee table and opened the voice recorder app. He had recorded thirty-three minutes of audio. Muting the television, he pushed play and listened with the volume turned up loud. At first, he heard nothing, and he didn't know whether to feel relieved or disappointed. Then the disorganized sound of static rose from the recording. He couldn't figure out where that could have come from. There would be no reason for static to happen on the recording.

There was nothing on in the house. The static continued for ages and grew louder and louder until Adam had to turn down his phone afraid he would blow out the speaker. He stopped the recording and thought for a few minutes. He needed to find out what he was listening to. He pushed play again and listened some more, this time with the volume turned down. The wall of static started opening revealing something else, possibly words. He rewound it a few seconds and listened again. He was hearing something. The static stopped almost as suddenly as it began, and he could hear voices. Lots of voices talked to each other as if in a crowded room. Silverware clinked against plates and glasses. Jazz played in the background. It was like he was listening to a party. The conversations were too muddled for him to make out. The voices rose and fell together as if on cue. Sometimes he picked out laughter. When the recording was over, he rewound it and listened again.

He listened to the full thirty-three minutes of tape twice before Jules and Tim finally came home. "Are you all right?" Jules asked concern etched on her face.

He shook his head, "Just tired I guess."

"If you're too tired to drive home you can sleep here," Tim said.

Adam was grateful for the invitation. He was going to ask anyway. He lay in their guest room that night looking at the ceiling and thinking about the recording on his phone. When he got home, he would try to make another, but tonight he would rest confident a ghost wouldn't wake him in the night.

CHAPTER TEN

CHERYL woke before the sun. The night sky was only just beginning to find the colors of daylight. She stood looking out her bedroom window, her hair in a messy braid. She took a few sips of the milky coffee in her oversized yellow mug and looked out at the sleeping city street. The caffeine hadn't yet kicked in, and her thoughts were groggy. She was up much earlier than she needed to be, but sleep had not come easily the night before. After only a few hours of rest, she woke again in the dark hours of early morning and lay in her bed frustrated. Finally, she gave up and decided to get out of bed, her stomach aching from the ice cream she'd eaten last night.

Even though she was exhausted, she kept telling herself it was good to get an early start. She would need to find someplace to read to replace the hours she was doing at the Starlight Café. That should have been her top priority, but she kept thinking about the mysterious couple she had seen in Adam's kitchen. Their obsidian eyes were like black holes sucking in all the light around them. Just thinking about them made her quake with fear. She wondered how Adam survived living in the apartment with them for so long. Surely, she would not have the strength to do the same. She took the last sip of her coffee. The warm liquid in her mouth helped to wake her. She padded out to the living room on bare feet. The sun had climbed high enough in the sky to send streams of dusty light through the open blinds in the living room. One of those strips of light landed squarely on the black phone on the end table, the red blinking light atop reminding her of the voicemail she had yet to listen to. Cheryl continued into the kitchen and refilled her mug with coffee. The blinking light on the phone was like a finger poking her. She could feel it even through the plaster of the wall, demanding her attention.

Armed with a fresh cup of coffee, she went back into the living room and gently removed the phone from its cradle. She set her mug on the end table and dialed the number to listen to the new messages.

"You have one new message," the mechanical voice on the other end said. "To listen to your messages, press one."

Cheryl took the phone away from her ear. She considered hanging up and not listening to the message, but she had done that already the day before. There was a small chance it was something important. With a shaky finger, she pressed one and tentatively put the phone to her ear.

"First message," the voice said.

A low moaning creak eased through the telephone. It started out soft and slowly grew in volume. When Cheryl was about to take the phone away from her ear, it stopped. "Hurry. We won't last much longer," the same childish voice she'd heard on her phone before said. "Help us."

A jolt of cold shot through her and Cheryl dropped the phone. It clattered on the floor. Her heart rose into her throat and seemed to swell so large that it might choke her. She swallowed hard and let out a few wheezing breaths. A wave of dizziness washed over her. She grabbed hold of the arm of the chair to steady herself. She had almost convinced herself the other phone calls had happened in a dream. Maybe this was all a dream, and none of it was real. That was what she wanted to believe but wanting it didn't make it true.

Clamping her eyes closed, she took some steady, controlled breaths as she tried to regain her balance. Part of her was hoping that when she opened them, she would be somewhere else. She would still be in bed having just awoken from a terrible nightmare. She opened her eyes only to find herself in the living room. The creaking sound started again. It grew like a weed from the telephone and spread through the air. Even with the phone on the floor, she had to cover her ears. "Stop!" Cheryl yelled. The sound continued, overpowering her. She cupped her hands over her ears and dropped to her knees. "Leave me alone! I don't know what you want!"

Just when she thought the sound was so loud it might deafen her, it stopped. Cheryl unfurled herself from the ball she'd curled into. Sitting on her knees on the hard floor, she reached over to the phone and hung it up. She leaned over, grabbed her coffee from the end table, and downed the whole mugful in one giant gulp. She would need all the energy she could get if she was going to figure out what was going on.

Cheryl did her best to go about her morning routine as if nothing had happened. She knew that was the only way she would be able to get anything done. Otherwise, she would end up hiding in the corner of her closet sobbing all day. There was no time for that. She needed to get work done if she wanted life to continue as usual. The list of tasks to complete was long. She had to find some extra income. She had to solve the mystery of her strange phone calls and Adam's haunting. She knew she wouldn't get any of that work done in her place. She'd be too worried. Cheryl took her computer to the library where she could work on solving some of these problems. She decided to start with public records to see if she could find anything unusual about Adam's apartment.

Cheryl spent most of the morning looking for answers about Adam's ghosts. The couple she'd seen haunted her thoughts and wondering about them took her mind off her problems. She scoured the internet looking for information about the plot of land Adam's building stood on. When she didn't find anything, she remembered the haunting hadn't started there. Looking up information about his apartment was useless. It had started at the first house he rented. She knew she'd jotted down the address when he'd told her about the house. It only took a few minutes of searching through her bag to find the scrap of paper she'd written it on. Armed with the address, she decided to look up the property to see what she could find out about it.

The house was built in 1964, making it the newest home on that block. A bit more digging led her to a little website that belonged to a Florida historical society.

It was very bare bones and looked like it had been set up twenty years ago and never touched again. Buried in the pages of the website Cheryl found what she was looking for, a grainy black-and-white picture of a boxy two-story house where Adam's old rental now stood. Even though the house dwarfed the others on either side of it, its architecture was underwhelming. Simple and square with a sharply pointed roof, it stood toward the back of the lot away from the sidewalk like a shy child. Cheryl leaned into her computer screen to get a closer look. Darkness seemed to ooze from the house. Boards covered the windows, and dark parasitic vines crawled up the home's face. The house brought up more questions than it answered. She needed to find out who lived in it. If she could find the answer to that question, she'd probably know who was haunting Adam.

It was already noon. Cheryl had to leave the library to get to the Italian restaurant where she and Stephanie had agreed to meet. She bookmarked the page on her computer, packed up her things and headed out the door. Stephanie was easy to spot sitting outside at the Italian place on Beach Drive. Her long dark hair hung over the back of her chair, and her bright red blouse billowed in the breeze. Cheryl always felt a bit plain in comparison. Stephanie's makeup was perfect, sharp black liner and cherry-red lips. Cheryl was lucky if she managed to put on some mascara in the morning and a tinted lip balm. No matter what, by the end of the day the mascara would be smudged.

Cheryl sat down. "I feel underdressed," she said. Clothes were the last thing on her mind when she left the house, and it was only when she saw Stephanie that she realized she was wearing paint-stained capri pants and a faded old T-shirt.

"You've got a look going there," Stephanie said. "I would call it hobo chic."

Feeling embarrassed, Cheryl didn't laugh.

"Don't worry about it," Stephanie said, noticing her discomfort. "This is Florida, everyone looks like a bum."

"That doesn't make me feel any better." Cheryl opened the menu and started trying to decide what to order.

"Lighten up. No one cares what you're wearing. I'm just dressed like this because I'm working today." Stephanie took a sip of her ice tea. "What's going on with you? You seem stressed every time we talk."

Cheryl closed her menu and looked up at Stephanie. "To start, Connie fired me from the Starlight Café."

"She can't fire you. Technically you don't work for her."

"Didn't ... It's her business, and she has the right to tell me I can't do readings there anymore."

"What happened? I thought that was working out."

"There was a bit of a mix-up about whether or not I was supposed to be paying for the coffee. I thought I wasn't. She thought I was. It was an honest mistake. I wasn't trying to get one over on her or anything. I even offered to pay her for them, but she asked me to leave anyway. She said there's a lot of stuff going on right now and she thought it would be better if I didn't do readings there anymore."

Stephanie shook her head. "That's ridiculous, but you'll find someplace else. Haven't you been getting a lot of work through that psychic phone network?"

Cheryl nodded. "Yeah, but I'd rather do readings in person."

"You should go around to all the cafés to find out if anyone else will let you read there, just like Starlight did. To be honest, I don't like that place anyway. Damon's ex used to be a barista there. I try to ignore it, but I don't think he's over her yet. Sometimes I see him staring off into space, and I think he might be thinking about her."

"That sucks."

"Sure does. Especially considering that I'm hopeful this will get more serious. I just need to give him some time. She dumped him pretty hard, so I don't think there's any chance of them getting back together."

The waiter came over to take their orders before Cheryl was ready. Because Stephanie was in a hurry, Cheryl just picked a random thing on the menu and hoped it would be good. She'd eaten at the restaurant before but hadn't remembered what she'd ordered.

"Is this thing with Connie all that's been going on with you?" Stephanie asked.

"No. There's been a lot of weird stuff going on. I don't even know if I should tell you about it because you might think I need to be locked up."

Stephanie raised an eyebrow. "Have you committed a crime?"

"No." Cheryl shook her head. "I mean locked up in a mental hospital."

Stephanie cackled. "I already know you're crazy. I am too. That's why we're friends. So, you might as well just tell me what's been going on."

Cheryl told her about the phone calls at her place. She decided to save the Adam story for later.

"Maybe the wires are just getting crossed. Isn't that something that happens with landlines?" Stephanie fiddled with the gold bracelet on her wrist.

"Crossed lines don't happen anymore." Every time Cheryl thought about the phone calls a sick feeling opened in the pit of her stomach. "I think that's an old-fashioned problem that only happened when they first made telephones."

"I guess you're an old-fashioned girl with old-fashioned problems."

Cheryl rolled her eyes.

"It sounds like prank phone calls to me. It's probably just kids messing around trying to scare you."

Cheryl hadn't thought about the possibility, but it did make sense. It was the most reasonable way to explain these calls. They were just sounds that could've been recordings. The voice she heard was obviously a child. "You're probably right." Cheryl was trying to convince herself. "Since you have reasonable explanations for everything, maybe you can explain the ghosts I saw."

"Sorry, I can't do that," Stephanie said. "What time period do you think they were from?"

"I'm no expert, but I would guess the forties."

"Have you looked at the history of that piece of land. I know the buildings are new, but there must have been something else there before?"

"The haunting didn't start there. He's been having problems with these ghosts for about a year. I looked into the property where it all first started. I found a picture of the house that used to be there just before I came here."

"What's it look like?"

"It's a big old place that looks like it would be haunted. The picture I found was a grainy black and white taken in the fifties. The house looks like it's been abandoned for years." Cheryl pulled her laptop out of her bag and set it on the table. "I'll show you."

She found the picture quickly. Stephanie didn't look at it long. "I don't like the looks of that place. I swear it's going to give me nightmares." She turned the computer around, so it was facing Cheryl again.

"I know, right?" Cheryl took one last look at the old house before shutting her laptop down.

"Something terrible happened in that place."

"I have my suspicions," Cheryl said. "I was thinking I might find something else about it in the reference section at the library."

"The reference section? You're so old school. I'm sure you'll have more success looking for information online."

Cheryl sighed. "What I need to do is find someone who lived in the neighborhood when the house was still there and find out what they know. I'm sure a house that looked like that has some kind of urban myth attached to it."

Stephanie smiled. "I think I know someone who could

help you. One of my neighbors who lives across the street is like one million years old. She's lived here forever. Maybe she knows something. I can ask her next time I see her."

Cheryl had nothing to lose. "That would be good."

It wasn't very likely that talking to Stephanie's neighbor would lead to anything, but Cheryl didn't want to leave any stone unturned. She felt the only way to get the couple out of her head was to figure out who they were and how Adam could get rid of them. When she agreed to help him, she hadn't realized she would get so caught up in it.

CHAPTER ELEVEN

SHE wanted to meet at the Starlight Café. Cheryl tried to suggest someplace else, but she was insistent. When Cheryl arrived, the café was busy. The line of people waiting to order almost reached the door. She put her head down, letting her black hair fall like a curtain across her face, and hurried by the counter hoping not to be recognized. She used to love coming to the café, but now Connie had asked her not to do readings there she felt like she could never return. Despite the line to the door, there was a scattering of empty tables. Cheryl spotted Betty easily. She was the oldest person in the place. A halo of tightly curled lemon-yellow hair framed her small pruned face. Cheryl made a beeline to her table.

"Betty?" she asked the woman.

Her watery blue eyes brightened beneath hooded eyelids. "You must be Cheryl. Stephanie described you to me, but she didn't do you justice."

Cheryl pulled up a chair and sat down with her back to the rest of the coffee shop. The last thing she wanted was to be recognized.

"Stephanie tells me you're a psychic or something. I must have you read my future." She laughed and reached across the table touching Cheryl's hand. "Not that an old broad like me has much of one."

"Don't say that. I'd love to read your cards sometime. I can't do it here, though." Cheryl twisted in her chair looking at the scene behind her briefly. She wondered if Connie was there. She turned around and leaned back across the table toward Betty. "I used to read people's tarot cards here several times a week, but the owner asked me to stop."

Betty nodded knowingly. "I thought I'd seen you before. I'm not very good with faces." She was small and hunched. Her face was so close to the tabletop that when she took a sip of coffee, she barely had to lift the cup to get it to her lips. "You're not ordering anything?"

Cheryl shook her head. "I'd rather not. I still feel a bit embarrassed about the whole situation. It was only a couple days ago."

Betty put her coffee cup down on her saucer and opened her mouth in disbelief. "No wonder you didn't want to meet here. You kept suggesting other places. I was wondering what was wrong with the Starlight Café? Everyone loves the Starlight."

"I used to love it here too," Cheryl said. "I probably will again once I get over this whole thing." Cheryl's foot bounced beneath the table as she spoke. She didn't think showing up in the café again would make her nervous, but it had.

"Time heals all wounds."

"That's what they say." Cheryl thought about the scar on her abdomen from the time her ex-husband stabbed her with a kitchen knife one drunken night. She could still remember the way the knife burned as it entered her flesh, pushing aside skin and muscle. Her mind seemed to shut off, and the world around her became blinding white heat. So many years later, and the flesh in that spot was a mound of shiny unnaturally smooth skin that still ached sometimes at night. She thought about how jumpy she could sometimes be when she was alone with a man, and how she couldn't bring herself to trust anyone. Some wounds never heal no matter how much time passed.

"Stephanie said you had some questions for me." Betty gripped the edge of the table and scooted up in her chair. When she did the chair tipped up slightly. The back leg hit the floor hard.

Cheryl jumped up from her seat and reached across the table.

"Even if I did fall you wouldn't be able to catch me from there." Betty cleared her throat and sat up as straight as her hunched back would allow.

As Cheryl sat down, she looked around to see if anyone was looking at them. No one was. Everyone in the café was too involved in their own worlds to notice anything Cheryl did.

"You get to be in your eighties, and suddenly your biggest fear is falling. If I slipped and hit the ground, I don't know if I would be able to survive." Betty snorted. "I was a gymnast when I was a kid. I was one of those little girls bouncing all over the place like a Mexican jumping bean. I loved doing the floor routines, but the parallel bars were my specialty. I couldn't support my weight on those bars now if my life depended on it." She got a faraway look in her eyes. "Those were the days. Too bad I had to quit. I got to be too tall to compete professionally. If you're too tall, it throws off your center of gravity. Looking at me now, you'd never guess I was ever too tall for anything, right?"

Cheryl raised an eyebrow at her. "I wasn't going to say anything."

"I shrank. Osteoporosis can do a number on your height. I'll never be able to ride a rollercoaster again." She smiled and took another sip of her drink.

"You're not that short."

"Yes, I am. I can't get onto Space Mountain." Her eyes twinkled as she took another sip of her coffee.

Cheryl felt like Betty was waiting for her to say something, but she wasn't sure what.

Betty wiped her face with her napkin smudging her pink lipstick. "Okay, you caught me. That's an exaggeration."

Cheryl smiled. "I had no idea."

"Have you been to Disney World?" Before Cheryl could answer, she added. "Or is it Disney Land? I don't know the difference."

Cheryl shook her head. "I haven't been to either. I'm partial to water parks. I like the slides, but regular amusement parks aren't my thing. Once I went to a Great Adventure, and my friends coaxed me into getting on a roller coaster that goes upside down. It was a nightmare, and I lost my house key. It fell right out of my pocket. It wasn't a big deal because it was just the house key. I was a teenager and didn't have any other keys, but it was a bummer. Then we went on the Viking. You know that ship that rocks back and forth. I thought I was going to throw up on that thing. That would've been a disaster. I wonder if anyone has thrown up on it. I bet they have. How could they not? The only rides I remember liking were the Roaring Rapids and the Log Flume. There's just something about water that makes a ride five thousand times better."

Betty looked at her blankly and blinked a few times. "What was it you wanted to ask me, dear?"

"Yeah, of course. I don't want to keep you too long." Cheryl pulled her tablet out of her purse and brought up a picture on the historical website she'd found before. She slid it across the table to Betty. "I was just wondering if you knew anything about this house."

Betty pushed her coffee to the side and squinted down at the tablet. "I can't see the picture."

"You can pick it up." Cheryl reached over, tilting the tablet up to her. "Take it."

"I don't want to break it."

"Don't worry; you won't. I've dropped that thing more than I'd like to admit and it's still working."

Betty took the edge of the tablet cautiously in her fingers and pulled it closer to her face. "Where was this house?"

Cheryl rattled off the address.

"I remember the place. I grew up right around the corner from there." She looked at Cheryl over the tablet and a dreamy smile spread across her face.

"I'm so glad you remember it." Cheryl knew that asking Betty about the house was a long shot. She'd expected their meeting to be fruitless. This was a pleasant surprise. "What can you tell me about it?"

"Before they let that place fall into ruin it was owned by a wealthy couple from up north. This whole area was just vacation places for the rich in the winter." She chuckled. "I guess it still kind of is. My family always lived here full-time."

"Do you know anything about the couple who lived there?"

Betty laid the tablet back on the table. "My family didn't run in those circles, but we heard all the rumors. There were always so many rumors about the people in those big houses. That was before TV, and we needed something to keep us entertained."

"Did you hear rumors about the people who lived in this house?" Cheryl asked.

A smirk slid across Betty's face, and mischief sparked in her eyes. "The Butler's lived in that house. They walked around like they thought they were better than everybody else. Even the other rich folks didn't like them." She scooted forward in her chair, leaning into the table. "Rumor has it Mr. and Mrs. Butler weren't Mr. and Mrs. at all. They'd moved down here from New Jersey because they didn't know anyone here and could make up any blooming thing they wanted. Mr. Butler went around town flaunting his money, buying all kinds of cars and clothes, but it wasn't his money he was flaunting. It was his wife's, the real Mrs.

Butler. She was the one with the money. He'd never done an honest day's work in his life. He lived off his wife who, rumor has it he and the fake Mrs. Butler had institutionalized. I don't know how they did it. I don't even know if it was true."

"What happened to them?"

Betty pursed her lips and looked down at the table. "Nobody knows what really happened. The maid came into work one morning and found them both dead. The police investigation concluded it was a murder-suicide, but I don't know the details. After that, nobody wanted to buy that house. It sat abandoned for years. While people were living it up in the neighboring houses on the block, that one wasted away." A group of senior women came into the coffee shop. They waved at Betty, and she waved back.

"Your friends?" Cheryl said.

"I hope I'm giving you what you need because the bridge crew is here, and I'm ready to play."

Cheryl didn't realize Betty had an appointment after meeting with her. She was hoping she would have more time to talk. "Do you remember the Butlers' first names?"

Betty bit her bottom lip as she thought. "I'm not sure, but I want to say, Charles and Mary. No, that's not right. Miriam maybe."

"Charles and Miriam," Cheryl repeated.

"I think that's right."

"That's good for now. Would you have some more time to talk to me if I need to find out something else?"

"For you, my dear, I'd make time." A few of Betty's friends came over to the table balancing coffee cups on saucers.

Cheryl stood. "Thanks so much for taking the time to talk to me. I appreciate it."

Cheryl was so happy to get the information from Betty that she almost forgot she was trying not to be noticed by the coffee shop staff. She kept her head slightly turned away from the counter as she walked out the door hoping no one would recognize her. When she got out onto the street, she looked back through the large picture window at the front of the shop to see Betty's gaggle of friends joining her at the table. Laughing, their hands waved excitedly around their faces as they talked.

Goosebumps rose on Cheryl's arms in the cool breeze. She hiked the strap of her oversized-purse up further on her shoulder. She would go straight home and look up the Butlers. She wanted desperately to see a picture of them to find out if they were the couple she saw in Adam's apartment.

CHAPTER TWELVE

Influential Couple
Found Dead in Their Home

Horror rocked St. Petersburg when the bodies of Charles and Miriam Butler were found dead in their home on Wednesday morning. The couple's housekeeper, Patricia Spector, stumbled upon the scene when she arrived at work early that morning.

"It was terrible. I was so shocked I nearly fainted," Spector told the St. Petersburg Times. "The Butlers were good people. They didn't deserve this. No one does."

Both victims were shot. Charles Butler suffered a shot to the chest, and Miriam was shot in the head. Their wounds killed them instantly.

The Butlers moved to St. Petersburg from Melville, New Jersey five years ago. They were known for their lavish parties.

Police suspect this was a botched robbery attempt. "Whoever did this is a danger to the safety of our city. If you know anything about this crime we ask that you come forward immediately," Officer White of the St. Petersburg Police Department said.

The suspect continues to be at large. The police ask that all citizens take precautions until the suspect is apprehended. Keep your doors locked and don't let strangers into your home.

Cheryl studied the grainy black-and-white image to the left of the article. The couple in it looked as ghostly as they'd appeared in Adam's living room. The woman wore a beaded black dress. Large eyes peered out of her drawn face. A slender white cigarette dangled casually from her fingers. Her dark hair was cut into a sharp bob. The man's pinstriped suit hugged his square body too tightly. His deep-set eyes gave him a mysterious old-world look. Cheryl was sure the people in the photo were the same that she'd seen in Adam's apartment.

She was sitting at the table finishing up her third read of the article when her phone began to vibrate. It was Adam. "Hello."

"Are you okay?" His voice was almost a whisper.

"Yeah." Cheryl stared at the picture of the Butlers in front of her. "I was just getting ready to call you."

"But I beat you to it." She could hear the smile creeping into his voice, and it made her smile too.

"I found your ghosts."

"I know. That's what I was calling about."

Initially, she was jarred by his response, but then she realized what he meant. "I mean I found out who they were." She told him about her meeting with Betty and recounted everything she'd just read in the article.

"Does this mean you'll come back?" There was a longing in his voice that made her uncomfortable.

She hesitated. "Yes."

"Good." The tension drained from his voice. "When you ran out of here the other day I was sure you'd never come back." He let out a long exhale. "I've hired a lot of people, and most of them just ripped me off. They couldn't find anything, or they'd claim to feel a presence, but I could tell they were lying. You were the first one to feel them like I do, and the only one who saw them."

"They showed themselves to me. It wasn't because of anything I did."

"You have a special sense. The other people I hired pretend to know what they're doing. Maybe they've read a bunch of books about it or watched a bunch of ghost hunter shows. They were going through the motions, but you have a gift. It's real to you."

He sounded so convincing that for a moment she even agreed. "You are too kind. I didn't do anything special."

"You don't have to do anything special. That's what I'm

saying. You are special, so they came to you."

Cheryl shook her head. "I'm not special. I just try my best. I want to do a good job."

"That makes you special because most people don't try at all."

"I don't believe that."

"You don't deal with enough people then."

"I deal with people all day."

"None of this matters." He was ready to move on. "I want to know how to get rid of the Butlers."

Cheryl cleared her throat. "From the story I read, I think they are not at peace and might need help finding their way out of this world." A lump started to raise in Cheryl's throat. She was moving into unfamiliar territory and didn't like acting like she knew more than she did.

"Why are they in my condo? Shouldn't they have stayed in the other house?"

"I can't say for sure. Maybe they followed you because you were the first person to notice them." She smirked. "It looks like you're the special one."

"I don't want to be this kind of special." He paused, and she could hear him breathing into the phone. "Shouldn't they be following you now? You saw them."

Cheryl looked at the phone sitting on the side table next to her couch and wondered for a moment if Adam's ghosts were the ones calling her. "I guess." A black hole seemed to open in her chest as her senses went on high alert. Maybe she wasn't alone. "Has anything weird happened at your place since I was there?"

"It's gotten worse. What is with their fascination with

the shower? When I got home from work, the shower was on, and the air conditioner was cranked to forty degrees. It was like an icebox in here."

"I'm sorry. I was hoping they'd go because I saw them. I guess it's not that simple." Cheryl swallowed hard. She didn't want to go back to his apartment. She didn't want to feel that uneasiness again. "I'll come back, but I don't know what I'll do to help."

"Good," his voice brightened. "Can you come now?"

Cheryl could hear his expectant breathing on the other end of the phone. She didn't want to go back there, but she hated knowing she could've helped someone and chose not to. "Okay. I'll be there as soon as I can."

"Thank you," he said.

When she hung up, dread spread over her like ink. She slipped the phone into her bag and walked over to Adam's apartment.

"I've got something I want you to hear," he said.

"What?"

Adam walked into his living room assuming Cheryl would follow close behind. She hesitated before stepping over the threshold. She reached into her pocket and rubbed the smooth blue stone she kept there. He picked his cell phone up from the coffee table. "I recorded the room when I was in the shower."

"They showed up on video."

"Not video. Just audio. I should've recorded a video. I noticed the voice recorder on the phone and thought I'd see if they had anything to say. I left it recording on the kitchen table, and when I came back, there was something on it. I've done it twice now, and both times I got something different. The first recording sounded like it was just a party."

"The article I read about them said they liked to throw lavish parties," Cheryl said.

"That means we're on to something, right?"

"If you have a recording of them that's almost as good as seeing them."

"That's why I tried to record them again. Check this out. It's the recording I made today." He opened the app and pushed play. There were a few clicking sounds, then footsteps and the sound of a door closing. Then nothing.

She looked up at him. His jaw tightened. His eyes flicked back and forth between the phone and her face.

"Is something going to happen?" she tapped her foot on the ground. Her blood strained against her artery walls in anticipation.

"Wait."

She looked at the time on his phone. It was two forty-five. They stood together listening to the silence. They both stared at the screen watching the red dot inch its way up the white line. "Maybe you should speed it up or something—"

A burst of static crackled through the tiny cell phone speaker. Cheryl jumped and grabbed hold of Adam's forearm.

"This is it," he said. "Listen to this."

Cheryl looked up from the phone to see him looking down at her. His gaze was so expectant it scared her. "Just listen," he said.

She strained trying to hear something, anything significant, but all she heard was white noise. "I don't know what I'm listening for."

"Shhsh."

She looked at him, and he motioned for her to look at the phone as if looking at it could make her hear better.

"Can you hear it?" he asked.

She shook her head.

He frowned and ran the recording back a bit. "Listen to this part. Underneath the static, you can hear a voice. I think it's a woman." He pressed play again.

Now she knew what she was listening for she thought she could hear lumbering words intermingled with the haze of white noise, but what was it saying? "Run it back again." She leaned down, putting her ear closer to the phone so she could hear.

He pressed play again. "You betrayed me," he said.

Cheryl looked up at him.

"You will pay," he said.

Cheryl's blood ran cold. Her ex-husband had said those same words to her more times than she could count. She stood up straight, and her body began to tremble with fear. "What?" She crossed her arms over her chest and took a few steps away from him already planning her escape.

"That's what the voice is saying." He looked over at her and furrowed his brow. "Are you okay?"

Cheryl took a few steadying breaths. She couldn't freak out. Adam was not Carl. He was not going to do anything to her. "Yeah, I'm fine."

"Listen." He looked back at the phone.

Cheryl returned her attention to the recording. Now she could hear it too. The words were slurred, but they were definitely there.

"Do you think that was Mrs. Butler?" she asked. She looked up at him to see him put his finger to his lips telling her to be quiet.

The static fell away, revealing two distinct voices. "Do what you want!" the man said. "Why would you think it mattered that much to me anyway?"

"Good," the woman said. "I will."

A solid bang came through the speaker like someone dropping a plank of wood on concrete. Then there was silence. Adam stopped the recording.

"Where did you record this?"

"I left the phone in the kitchen on the table while I showered. I wanted to make sure I did the same thing I did when I got the first recording."

Cheryl walked into the kitchen. The room still swam with dread. The feeling that someone was standing too close behind her crept into her consciousness, but when she turned around Adam was on the other side of the room.

"What is it?" he asked.

She shook her head. "Nothing. I just felt like someone was behind me."

"Can you see them?"

Cheryl looked around the room. "Nothing other than what you can see."

Adam let out an exhausted sigh. "Can you make them show up, so we can find out how to get them out of here?"

"I've already told you it doesn't work that way. I don't

know what I'm doing." Remembering her purse, she opened it and pulled out her tarot cards. "I thought I'd try starting where I left off last time." She put the deck of cards on the table.

"Good." The chair legs squealed as he pulled it out and motioned for her to sit down.

Cheryl lowered herself into the wooden chair. The cards slid out of the box, falling into her hand. The heft of them comforted her as the air seemed to churn with foreboding. Shuffling the deck, she thought of the couple she'd seen standing in the kitchen. Their translucent forms tattooed on her memory. She rapped the deck on the table to straighten it before looking up at Adam who was glancing around the room as if looking for the wispy evidence of ghosts. "This should work," she said. She didn't know if it would but thought that saying so would make it more likely.

She laid the cards on the table in her favorite pattern, the Celtic cross. She felt Adam's eyes on her as she put each card on the smooth hard surface. When she finished, she looked up at him. "Here goes nothing." She reached out to turn the first card over, but before her fingertips could touch the card, it flipped over on its own. Cheryl's heart raced. She didn't want to believe any of this. Somewhere deep inside she kept hoping she'd find out none of it was true. She would've much rather found out she was losing her mind than think ghosts might be real.

"Did you see that?" Adam's voice was breathy.

Cheryl nodded. "How could I not?"

"Are you there?" Adam asked. He walked into the middle of the kitchen and stood there for a few moments waiting. When only silence answered him, he asked again, "What do you want from me?"

Cheryl looked at the card that was revealed on the top of the spread. A golden structure stood tall against a blue background. Flames leaped from the top of the building, and a bolt of lightning harpooned the top of the structure. "The Tower," Cheryl whispered.

Adam spun around, so he was facing her. "What?"

"That's the name of the card."

"What's it mean?" He walked back over to the table to get a look at the card.

"There's going to be a big change. Something will shake up the foundation of your belief."

"That's already happened." He gave a dry laugh that sounded more like a cough.

"It's already happened to me too." She thought about how quickly her life had changed in the past few days. She'd lost her work at the Starlight Café. She'd seen a ghost. She'd been getting those terrible phone calls. "Considering what just happened. I think we've got even more of a shakeup to look forward to."

"I'm pretty sure 'to look forward to' is not the best way to put it." He leaned over, resting his hands on the table. "The funny thing is, I should be more freaked out about what just happened. I've gotten so used to stuff in here moving by themselves, it's starting to become normal."

"We have to be careful about what we think of as normal. I mean... I certainly don't want this to be normal."

"That goes without saying." He stood up straight again, looking across the kitchen at the place where the stove sat and said, "We know you're here, so tell us what you want."

Cheryl stared straight ahead too. Both watched and waited for something to happen. Anticipation rose in Cheryl's body like a tide. She gripped the edges of the table, her heart pounding in her chest. Beneath the sound of her heart, she could hear the low hum of the refrigerator, the sound of footsteps in the apartment above them, the whisper of the wind as it blew outside. "I don't think yelling at them is going to work. If you want to communicate with someone you need to start to be nice. You know... Empathize with them, put yourself in their shoes, let them know you understand how they feel. That's when people open up to you. I know, I took an online class once. It was called How to Talk to Anyone. It was super useful. Before I took it, I was unbelievably shy and had no confidence. Now, look at me." She held her arms open wide. When she noticed Adam's scowl, she dropped them to her side again. She'd said too much. "I'm just saying those classes can be useful. If you have the discipline to study yourself, you can make a class like that work." Cheryl let her words trail off. She was rambling again. She often did that when she was nervous. "Sorry." She looked down at the tarot cards on the table, her face growing flush with embarrassment. "I talk too much in these situations. It makes it hard to believe I used to hardly talk at all, doesn't it?"

"Yep."

"Okay, sorry." She shook her head.

"Stop apologizing. I don't even know what you're apologizing for." He looked back up, and Cheryl was glad his eyes were off her. "We're still waiting for you to talk to us," he said into the air.

She returned her gaze to the back wall of the kitchen. She wanted so badly to say something else because speaking seemed to let the tension seep out of her, but she knew it was best for her to be silent. Ice-cold air danced across her fingertips, and she released the table edge from her grip. Just as she was about to ask Adam if he felt that too, the tarot cards rose from the table and flung themselves across the room. They landed on the floor in front of the stove like fallen leaves. Cheryl stood and sent her chair toppling over. It clattered on the tile floor.

"This is crazy." Adam rushed over and looked at the pile of cards on the floor.

Cheryl fought her instinct to dash out the door and down the stairs like she had before. Instead, she joined him in front of the tarot cards. She was half expecting them to be arranged into the shape of the word on the floor or to see a card of significance face up, greeting them. All the cards were face down. "What does this mean?"

"You're the professional. You're supposed to tell me."

She grabbed hold of her feather pendant she wore around her neck and started moving it up, and down the chain. She thought the motion would conceal her shaking hands. "Well, I guess we know they're here."

"They are always here, but does this mean they're willing to talk this time?" Adam squatted down and started picking up the cards.

Cheryl turned around a few times looking at every corner of the kitchen hoping to see them again. They were keeping themselves hidden. "Mr. and Mrs. Butler, I'm sure you remember me. I'm the one who you showed yourself to not too long ago. I was reading about your life the other day. You're so very interesting. I wish I had the opportunity to know you when you were alive ... I mean when you lived here. You gave some tremendous parties and were the toast of the town. Is that what you said back then 'toast of the town'? It doesn't matter. Anyway, I think you might be hanging around Adam's place because you have some kind of problem, or maybe have something to tell him. As you could see from what happened before, I can see you and maybe even talk to you. Anything you have to say you can tell me. I'm trustworthy enough, and Adam hired me to see if we can help you."

Adam looked up at her and raised an eyebrow.

"You can't get someone to open up to you if you don't build a foundation of trust first," she whispered to him as if whispering would keep the ghosts from hearing her.

Adam stood and handed her the pile of cards. "Did you learn that in your online class?"

"Sure did."

"I guess it was worth all the money you paid for it then."

"It was free and worth every dime." She winked at him. "I also learned if you ask a question you have to be willing to be quiet and let them answer."

"We're waiting for an answer." He looked at the ceiling.

Cheryl shook her head. "That's not how you do it. You just have to be quiet and listen. You don't want to make them feel pressured."

"No pressure here," Adam called toward the ceiling.

Cheryl couldn't help but giggle. It was better than the alternative. She liked that Adam could make her laugh in situations like this. They stood next to each other waiting for something to happen for a few long minutes. When nothing did, Adam looked at Cheryl as if to ask now what?

Cheryl shrugged. "Building trust takes time."

"I don't have time." He handed her the pile of cards.

"Thanks." Giving up, she walked back over to the table to return the cards to their box. As she approached the table, she felt the same cold air again spiraling around her. "Do you feel that?" She turned back to look at Adam and saw the Butlers standing beside him. Each had a wound the size of a quarter that seeped black blood. Miriam's sat at her temple; dark blood dripped down her ear. Charles's was in his chest, a black hole of grief. Though their forms flickered, like a television station that was not quite coming in, the pleading in their eyes was easy for Cheryl to recognize. She had felt that same desperation before she had sacrificed everything she'd ever known to run away to Florida.

She inhaled sharply. "They're right next to you. Can you see them?"

The couple turned their heads in unison to look at Adam as if Cheryl was asking them if they could see him.

Adam searched the room with his eyes. "Where are they?"

"Right there. Beside you." Cheryl raised a shaking finger and pointed.

The couple looked back at her, and the two of them raised their hands, their slim fingers pointing back at her.

Cheryl didn't know whether to laugh or run away. She took a few deep breaths and tried to organize her thoughts. "How do you talk to ghosts?" she asked Adam.

"You were the one who was just telling me about your communication class." He was still looking around the room like the more he looked, the more likely he'd be able to see something. "I guess you talk to them just like you'd talk to anyone else.

CHAPTER THIRTEEN

ADAM saw nothing, but he knew from the fear in Cheryl's eyes they weren't alone. His ghosts were there again, showing themselves to her. This time she wasn't going to run away. He wouldn't let her even if she tried. He'd block the exit and make her stay. He'd hold on to her, not letting her go. It was wrong, but he wasn't going to be left alone again. Now she'd seen the ghosts, they were connected. She seemed to know that too.

The fear drained from her eyes as she walked in his direction staring intensely at a spot on the wall. "Tell us what you want. We only want to help you." She glanced over at him. With every passing second, she seemed to gain confidence.

"Are they saying something?" he asked.

She held her finger to her lips. "Not yet."

Adam searched for them with his eyes but saw nothing. As he focused, he could feel them now, a pressure pushing on his right shoulder. "I want to know what I can do to help you move on." He looked at the empty air next to him. His blood ran cold as the pressure on his shoulder increased. He wanted to move, to run out of the room, but she was staying, and so would he. He usually stayed and knew if he willed himself, he was able to cope with the discomfort the spirits brought with them. He took a step to his left to put some distance between him and the spirits. The pressure in his shoulder decreased, and he took another step away from them, finding it decreased even more. "Are they saying anything?"

She held up her finger again.

It was hard to be quiet. He wanted to know what was happening. He fought his need to be in control and bit his tongue.

They stayed there quiet for what felt like forever. Adam's mind raced. The pressure on his shoulder increased again, and he walked away from it, standing next to Cheryl. He followed her gaze and looked at the same point on the wall she focused on. He saw nothing. Why did he see nothing? They had been destroying his life for months. Shouldn't they give him the courtesy of showing themselves to him?

Cheryl groaned, and he looked over just in time to see her head fall forward, her shoulders slump, her knees buckle. She tumbled to the floor. Adam reached for her, his arms encircling her just in time to cushion her fall. He laid her gently on the floor and looked at her face, her small nose a contrast to her full dark lips. Her eyes slid from side to side beneath her eyelids. Her muscles twitched. Adam knelt at her side. "Wake up," he said, nudging her shoulder, but she didn't respond.

The air in the room grew heavy. The pressure he'd previously felt on one shoulder spread across his entire body, like a lead apron being draped over him. "What's happening?" he said aloud.

Her face spasmed. This wasn't right. It wasn't what had happened before. He needed to get his phone to call the 911, but he couldn't move. His muscles strained and sweat beaded on his forehead. Was he dying too? He struggled to turn his head and focus on the spot Cheryl was looking at before she fell. He thought he saw pinpricks of light twinkling only a few feet from his eyes before floating away from him and vanishing. The weight lifted. Cheryl opened her eyes.

She focused on his face. "Why am I on the floor?" She eased herself up.

"Be careful." He placed his hand on the center of her back, helping her sit up. "You fell."

Cheryl let out a long sigh. Her shoulders slumped. "I'm exhausted."

"That's not surprising. I was afraid you were having a seizure." Relief washed over him. For a few brief seconds, he was certain they would both die. He moved closer to her wanting to give her a celebratory embrace. They were alive, but she shifted away from him.

She grabbed hold of the chair behind her and pulled herself up onto it. Adam wanted to help her but sensed he shouldn't.

He stayed on the floor, backing up so he could rest his back against the cabinet doors. She needed space, and he would give her whatever she needed.

"What did they say?" he asked.

She closed her eyes and breathed with her entire body for a few moments. When she opened them, calm replaced the confusion she'd felt just a few minutes earlier.

Words poured from her mouth, more than he ever expected. His eyes grew wide as he took them in. She did not stop speaking. She spoke and spoke, unfurling the story he had wanted to hear.

PART TWO

CHAPTER FOURTEEN

CHERYL rounded the corner and headed home in a world that wasn't the same as the one she'd woken up in. It was as if she were looking through different eyes. The sky was bluer, the sun brighter, and every object she passed gleamed. To anyone else at any other time, this would probably have seemed good, but it wasn't. It was wrong. The streets were more crowded than usual. Throngs of people pushed past her. She weaved through the crowd, wondering where they were all going. Was there a festival downtown? That would've been unusual on a weekday. She considered stopping to ask someone but didn't want to talk to anyone else today. She needed to get home to sort out her thoughts and figure out what had just happened to her. She moved back and forth through the crowd twisting her body to squeeze past people, muttering "excuse me" as she went. She was struggling to get past someone when she noticed a man standing on the corner looking at her and laughing. His light-colored shorts were baggy and stained. His T-shirt had so many holes, it was almost not a T-shirt at all. He raised a wobbling finger and pointed at her. He spoke revealing the gaping toothless hole that was his mouth. "What're you doing? Dancing?"

Cheryl ignored him and continued weaving through the crowd.

"Hey!" he called. "Lady, what on earth are you doing?" He laughed heartily, doubling over, and holding his stomach.

"Trying to get through this crowd," Cheryl finally said to him. She didn't think an explanation should be necessary. They were all going the opposite direction to her and walking against them was like swimming upstream. "Where are they all going?"

The man widened his eyes and shook his head, making a tutting sound with his teeth. "And they say I'm crazy."

Cheryl didn't pay him much mind because it was obvious to her that he was.

"There ain't hardly nobody there, but you." He pointed at the man in the gray business suit a few yards in front of her talking on the phone. "And him." He pointed to someone else, a small woman in a pink mini-skirt and white T-shirt. "And her."

Cheryl froze in her tracks. She looked at the two people he pointed at and then back at the man. There was no way what he was telling her was true. He lived on the streets and was obviously insane. He'd admitted it just a moment ago.

"That's all there is. Ain't no reason for you to do all that bobbing and weaving. You look like you're trying not to get shot by a sniper." His laughter bellowed in her direction. This time he collapsed to the ground completely. "This isn't

Iraq. You can calm down."

But as Cheryl stood there she could feel the crowd, all the bodies bumping against her, throwing her off balance. What he was saying couldn't be right. "Pardon me," she said to a young man brushing past her. His dark hair shone in the sun. "Where are you all going?"

The young man stopped in his tracks. Staring at her with joyful shock on his face, he asked, "Are you talking to me?"

Cheryl nodded. "Yeah. Where is everybody going?"

The young man clapped his hands together and smiled broader than Cheryl had ever seen anyone smile in her life. "I can't believe you can see me. Wait a minute. Are you dead, too?"

"What? No. Of course not." Even as she said it, she was starting to doubt. What had happened to her in Adam's apartment was intense, but there was no way it killed her. She had spoken to Adam before heading out the door. He'd asked her out. There was no way he would've done that if she were dead unless he was dead too.

"I need you to tell my sister I'm sorry. I should've been more careful. Tell her it wasn't her fault," the young man said.

"Who are you? Who is your sister?"

"Tamika Brown. I'm Andre. Tell her she was right. I shouldn't have been messing around that close to the edge. Tell her not to feel bad about it. There was nothing she could've done. I wouldn't have listened. I never listened. That was always my problem. I wish I had, but it's too late. Anyway, tell her it isn't her fault. It's mine. I'm sorry she had to see that, but she shouldn't feel guilty because she did everything she could to stop it from happening." His eyes shone with earnest intent as he talked to her.

Cheryl kept trying to right herself as the people pushed past her. "Okay." What was happening? Was this boy dead? Were all these people dead?

"Okay, what?" the man standing on the corner yelled at her. "It's getting worse. Now she's talking to herself."

Cheryl wished he'd stop talking and go away. She was trying to figure out what was going on and she was having a hard time doing that with all his yammering.

The young man told her an address. "That's where my sister lives. Go there and tell her what I told you."

Cheryl nodded. "I'll go there."

That wasn't good enough for him. "Repeat the address to me."

She did. "What am I going to do once I get there. She won't believe me. She'll think I'm a lunatic."

The young man thought for a moment. He looked at the crowd. Most of them had moved past now. "You're right," he said. "I'll have to go with you." He bit his lip like he was trying to make an important decision.

No one was jostling against them now. The crowd had thinned. "Where are they all going?"

"It's time. The light is that way." He nodded in the direction they were all heading. "The ones who are ready can move on now."

"You are dead then."

"I already told you that."

"I know. I was just making sure. It's not every day I

meet a dead person." He was so young. Cheryl thought that it was such a shame that his life had already ended.

"I'll go with you. That way she'll know it's real. Can we go now?"

Cheryl didn't want to go anywhere, but home. She couldn't do that though. He was only a teenager, and he needed her now. "Okay. We can go now. I'll have to get my car. It will be faster."

The boy smiled at her. "Thank you."

Cheryl's heart was racing as she pulled up to the curb outside of the little white wooden house with the chain-link fence around it. A blue bicycle lay abandoned on the sidewalk. Its silver spokes shone in the sun. She looked in the rearview mirror where she could see the young man sitting in the backseat, sadness reflected in his eyes. He looked out the window. "That's the place." Before Cheryl could say anything else, he vanished from the backseat.

She eased herself out of the car. Children played in the front yard across the street. Two little girls in cutoff shorts and T-shirts jumped rope on the sidewalk. The plastic rope clicked as it hit the cement. Their bodies bounced up and down effortlessly. The bangles on Cheryl's wrist jingled as she went up to the front gate. "What am I supposed to say?" she asked the air. "Andre? Where are you now?"

Before Cheryl could compose herself, the front door opened, and a sharp-faced woman stepped out. Her hair hung in thick braids that reached below her shoulders. Noticing Cheryl standing there with her hand on the gate, the woman said, "May I help you?"

Cheryl cleared her throat. "Um... Does Tamika live here?"

The woman narrowed her eyes and took a step forward placing her hand on her hip. "Who are you?"

Cheryl looked around hoping to see Andre again. He was there this time standing to her left. "Tell her you're her teacher's aide from school. I don't think she's ever met any of the teacher's aides."

"I'm a TA from school. I knew Andre, he was a good kid and I heard Tamika wasn't doing very well. I wanted to stop by to pay my respects." Cheryl lifted the latch on the gate and stepped into the yard. "I know this is a terrible time for you. I'll only take a few minutes of Tamika's time, Mrs.—"

"Brown," Andre said.

"Brown." Cheryl's heart was pounding so hard she wondered if Mrs. Brown could hear it. "May I speak to her?"

"Tamika!" Mrs. Brown glared at Cheryl, her arms crossed defensively as she called into the house.

A skinny brown-skinned girl slunk out onto the porch. Her hair was braided like her mother's. She looked at the ground, her arms crossed over her chest. "What?"

Mrs. Brown frowned. "Don't you say what to me."

"Sorry." She looked at the ground and stuck out her lip. "Yes." Her voice was soft, barely audible over the pounding of Cheryl's heart.

"That's better." Mrs. Brown put her arm around her daughter's shoulder pulling her close to her side and looked

Cheryl square in the eye. "You can say what you want to say now." She was distrustful, and Cheryl didn't blame her.

"I was hoping we could talk alone." Cheryl's mouth was dry.

"She's not going to let you talk to her alone." Andre was talking in Cheryl's ear making it difficult for her to concentrate. "Tell her I knew she was always trying to do her best to protect me. And tell her I'm sorry for all the times I was mean to her. I shouldn't have done that. Tell her it was my fault. I was acting a fool. I knew it too, but I thought it was funny. She knew how dangerous it was. She couldn't have done anything to stop it from happening. I slipped and fell because I was too hard-headed to listen."

Cheryl wanted to turn to him and ask how she was supposed to say all that and make it sound like it came from her, not him, but she had an audience. She couldn't turn around and talk to the air. She had to make something up on the spot that would make all this better. "I knew your brother at school. I work there." She didn't like lying but didn't see how else to do this.

"I've never seen you at school." Tamika's dark eyes were clouded with suspicion.

Cheryl couldn't blame her. She was acting suspiciously. "I'm only there part-time I work with the younger grades." Her throat was so scratchy she wondered if she could ask for a glass of water. "Your brother loved you."

"He told you that?" Mrs. Brown and Tamika said at once.

Realizing her story was going to sound a little far-fetched, Cheryl took a step back before continuing to speak.

"Not in so many words, but I could tell he cared about his family. He knew you were always trying to protect him because he was the youngest, and he appreciated that."

"I didn't do a good job of protecting him when it mattered." Tamika's voice cracked, and she put her hand over her mouth.

Mrs. Brown squeezed her shoulder. "We all know you did your best, baby. It wasn't your fault." She looked up at Cheryl. "Is that all you wanted to say?" Her voice noticeably harsher when addressing her.

"I guess. I just wanted her to know Andre knew what she did for him, and he appreciated it." This wasn't going the way she wanted.

Andre stood right next to her talking in her ear rapidly. "Tell her I'm sorry. Tell her I should've done better. Tell them I love them. Tell them I'm right here."

Cheryl cleared her throat. "He wants you to know it wasn't your fault. It was his fault. He was messing around and wasn't paying attention to what he was doing. He wishes it never happened too. Of course he does, but it has, and he doesn't want you to beat yourself up about it. You still have a life to live, live it. He wants you to remember him and live your life like you're living it for him too." Cheryl hoped she was getting it right. She wanted it to be right. She wanted to make everything better but looking at their faces, she couldn't tell. It was silent. Andre finally stopped speaking, and Mrs. Brown and Tamika stood on the porch staring down at Cheryl. Tears began streaming down both of their faces. Tamika fell to her knees and cupped her face in her hands.

"How could you possibly know what Andre wants?" Mrs. Brown knelt next to her daughter putting both her arms around her and holding her close. Tamika buried her head in her mother's chest, her body shaking with tears.

Part of Cheryl wanted to turn around and run away from all of this, but the young man next to her needed her to speak for him. How could she say no to that?

Mrs. Brown let go of her daughter and wiped the tears from her eyes. "What was your name again?"

"It doesn't matter," Cheryl said. "Andre wants you to know he loves you both. And he's grateful for all you did for him. That's all that matters. My role in all this is insignificant. I'm the messenger. He wants you to accept the message, so he can have peace." Cheryl still had the gate in her hand. She had been gripping it as she stood on the sidewalk that led up to their front porch. Now she was backing up pulling the gate closed, making her plans to escape. "I have to go now." She looked to her left to see Andre standing with his hands in his pockets nodding his head. His eyes were glassy too, but there were no tears on his cheeks.

"Thank you," he said to her.

She pulled the gate closed. "It was good meeting you." She put her hand up and waved sheepishly.

Mrs. Brown stood. "Wait," she called. She came down the front steps rushing up to the gate. Her high-heel sandals clopped against cement. "Why do you talk about my son like he isn't dead?"

Cheryl turned around to see her standing at the gate holding the top bar just as Cheryl had earlier. "I have to go."

She stepped around the bicycle and pulled the driver side door open.

"He's dead. We buried him a few days ago. I didn't see you at the funeral."

Cheryl didn't want to look at her tragic face again. She kept her head down. "I couldn't go. I'm sorry I couldn't be there, but I had some important family business to take care of." She started getting into the car. "My condolences." She wasn't even sure what that meant, but she knew you were supposed to say it to people when someone died. She pulled the car door closed and drove away slowly on the narrow street half expecting Andre to appear in the seat next to her. He didn't.

Once the Browns' house was out of sight, she pulled over, parking her car between a forest-green station wagon and silver SUV. Her heart thudding in her chest, she tried to take a deep breath, but when she exhaled a desperate sob escaped her mouth. She lowered her head on the steering wheel and began to cry, her body shook as it let out all the stress she'd felt these past few days.

Her crying session was interrupted by a gentle tap on her car window. Cheryl turned her head to see a round woman in a shapeless flowered frock standing outside of her window. Cheryl wiped the tears from her eyes with her hands before rolling down the window.

"Do you need help?" the woman asked.

"No. I'm sorry." When she was in her car it was easy for Cheryl to forget other people could see her. "I'm just having a strange day."

The woman pulled a travel package of tissues from the

pocket of her frock. "Take these."

Cheryl reached out and took the package.

"Man problems?"

Cheryl shook her head. "No. It's more complicated if that's even possible. I was just driving home, and I felt overwhelmed." Cheryl took a tissue from the package and blew her nose quietly.

"That happens sometimes."

They nodded at each other for a few moments neither saying anything.

"Change is usually a good thing, even if you can't see it at the time." The woman put her hands in her pockets. "Sometimes you need to be pushed into doing something that will make your life better."

"I don't know how this is going to make my life better." Cheryl thought about Mrs. Brown and Tamika standing on their front porch looking confused. "It might make everyone's live worse."

"You'll have to be creative then to figure out how to make it better." Her eyes sparkled, and she smiled. "You're smart. You'll figure it out."

"You don't know that."

"I'm an excellent judge of character," the woman said.

Cheryl tried to hand the package of tissues back to the woman.

"Keep them," she said. "I have plenty."

"Thank you." Cheryl looked at her lap, unsure of what to do next.

"You should get going. You have a lot to think about." The woman winked before stepping back away from the car. "Don't worry. You'll be fine." She walked around the back of the car and stepped up onto the sidewalk. Cheryl watched her through her rearview mirror as she walked up the street. Cheryl pulled away from the curb thinking about what the woman had said. She was going to be all right.

CHAPTER FIFTEEN

CHERYL had never imagined the world was so full of the dead. She passed one in the hall on the way back to her apartment. A woman in a royal-blue sundress hunched over in the corner talking to herself at the other end of the corridor. The crack in the wall behind her was visible through her transparent form. Cheryl hesitated before going into her apartment. Holding the key in her lock, she listened to the woman's incomprehensible muttering trying to decide whether to help her. Exhausted, she turned the key in the lock and went inside promising herself if she saw the woman again, she'd approach her.

She wondered if every ghost needed help like Andre. Was that why they were still here?

The landline started to ring. She looked at the phone sitting in the cradle on the table by the couch. She'd been avoiding it for the past few days, but a new-found courage bubbled up in her. She nearly tripped over the area rug as she ran over to pick up the phone. "Hello?"

A familiar crackling filled her ear, followed by the same

childlike voice. "Help us."

"I already know you need help. You have to tell me who you are and where you are. Otherwise, I can't help you." She spoke in a calm even tone that surprised even her.

Whoever was on the other end didn't answer. The crackling sound crescendoed. Cheryl strained to hear the voice beneath the noise.

"If you want help you have to give me some more information. If you don't and this is just some kind of crank you need to knock it off. This is my business line. I can't have you tying it up with these shenanigans." Cheryl laughed inside. She thought only people over seventy use the word shenanigans.

Whoever was on the other end hung up. The dial tone droned in her ear. "I guess it was a crank then," she said to herself, hanging up.

She walked over to the window and looked out. The sun was sinking in the sky, and the golden light filtering through the clouds made everything look a little bit better. It was almost time for her to log in to the Spirit Guides Network. She was still so shaken up by the events of the day she didn't know how well she'd be able to serve her clients.

"This is the psychic network. I'm Cheryl. What is the question you have for the cards?" It was her first call of the evening. She always needed a little bit of time to warm up, but this evening her head just wasn't in it. She hoped she could get more into the reading as it went on.

The person on the other end cleared her throat. "Is this the psychic?"

People referred to Cheryl as a psychic a lot, but she never really felt comfortable with the title. "I'm your tarot card reader for today. Do you have a question for the cards?"

The woman didn't say anything. Cheryl could hear some people talking on the other end of the line and assumed it was somebody joking around. She had gotten calls like that before, but as long as she kept the person on the phone, it didn't matter to the company.

Cheryl waited patiently for an answer. When the person didn't respond, she spoke again. "Are you coming up with a question?" She rapped her deck of tarot cards on the coffee table. "Most people want to know about their love lives or their finances. Are you having trouble in those areas?" She found some people needed to be helped along.

"Cheryl?" the woman asked.

"That's my name."

"This is going to sound a bit strange, but I've been getting these strange phone calls. The first one was just a whole lot of noise, like static or something. I thought the line was bad, so I hung up. But calls kept coming from the same number, and they were always the same ... lots of static. Then one day I answered, and I heard a child asking me for help."

Cheryl swallowed hard. Heat rose from her chest into her head, and she started to feel woozy. "I'm sorry, what did you say?"

The woman repeated herself almost word for word.

"The voice usually doesn't say much else besides 'help me,' but today, it told me to call this number. I normally wouldn't call a number like this. I'm annoyed I'm getting charged so much. Anyway, do you know anything about this? Or maybe it's a scam your company came up with to get people to call?"

Cheryl sat on her sofa, silent.

"Are you still there?" the woman asked.

Cheryl nodded and then realizing the woman couldn't see her said, "Yeah. Have you called the police?"

"I did, but when they tried to find out who the number belonged to, they found out it was unassigned. It didn't belong to anyone. Can you believe that? It seems like with all the phones in the world that every number should be taken, but not this one. Anyway, I think they thought I was a nutcase and dismissed me altogether. I haven't heard anything from them in a while."

As the woman was talking Cheryl wondered why she'd never considered calling the police herself. It was apparently something that was on her mind but why hadn't she done it? "That's strange."

"Anyway, I was hoping you would know something. I know it's a longshot but—"

"I know why you were told the call me." Her shoulders softened as she began to talk. Cheryl hadn't been able to talk about the phone calls she'd been getting, and finally sharing her story was a relief. "I've been getting the same phone calls on this number, my landline. Nobody knows this number except for the network."

"You're not just messing with me, are you? I mean if

you're getting the calls too that means I'm not crazy."

"That's exactly what I was thinking. I was starting to think I was losing my mind," Cheryl said.

"Why would the voice tell me to call you though? What does it want us to do?"

"I've been trying to figure that out."

"Can't your tarot cards tell you anything about this mystery?" the woman asked.

"No." Cheryl wasn't usually that quick to dismiss the cards, but she had a distinct feeling she needed to use another tool to solve this problem. She didn't know what though. "The call log says you're calling from here in St. Pete? Is that right, Sydney?" She read the woman's name from the display.

"Yeah."

"I'm in St. Pete too." Cheryl wanted to suggest they meet or give the woman her phone number, but that was not allowed. She was under contract to keep the call with the network and never offer any private meetings to clients. She was uncomfortable discussing this any further though because she knew someone would listen to this call later to make sure everything went well.

"I'm going to have to get off the line. This is already becoming more expensive than I can afford."

"There's a place here in St. Pete called the Starlight Café. Do you know it?"

"Yeah, I know it."

"According to what I see in the cards you should start going there tomorrow around lunchtime. The cards are telling me you'll be able to meet the person you've been looking for at the café."

"Do you mean we should—"

"I mean you will be able to meet the person you are looking for if you go to the café tomorrow at lunchtime."

"I understand."

"You'll find what you're looking for at the café."

"Thank you. Goodbye."

"Thank you for calling the Spirit Guides Hotline."

The woman hung up. Cheryl knew what she'd said was kind of obvious, but she was hoping no one would listen to the call too closely.

She'd have to make sure she looked like a psychic tomorrow and hoped Connie wouldn't be at the Starlight. She'd told the woman to meet her there out of habit. It was the first place that came to mind whenever she needed to arrange to meet someone.

The next call came in before she could think about much of anything else. She hoped meeting the woman tomorrow would help her figure out what was going on with the phone calls. Until then, she needed to take as many calls as she could to keep the money coming in. Her water bill would be due soon, and she needed to make paying the bills the priority.

The café wasn't busy, so Ruth saw Cheryl as she walked in. "Cheryl, it's so great to see you. After Connie asked you not to read here anymore, I was afraid I'd never see you again." She came out from behind the counter and hugged Cheryl.

Cheryl wasn't usually a big hugger, but she had been so nervous about coming into the café she was relieved to have such a warm reception. "How have you been?"

"Wonderful." Ruth smiled broadly. "The last reading you gave me was so accurate. I don't know how you do it. You have to give me another reading."

Cheryl looked around nervously. "I can't do it here."

"I know that. Give me a card so I can call you to make an appointment."

Cheryl fished a card out of her disorganized satchel purse and handed it to Ruth.

"Have you been busy since you left?"

Cheryl was still nervous. She looked over at the counter trying to see beyond it into the back.

Noticing, Ruth said, "Don't worry. Connie's not here today." She slid Cheryl's card into the back pocket of her black jeans. "You don't have to worry about her. I think she'd be happy to see you haven't stopped coming here just because she asked you not to do readings anymore."

"Honestly, I don't feel comfortable coming here anymore, but I arranged to meet someone. I always used to use this as my go-to meeting place, and I don't have any way to contact them to change it." Cheryl realized she didn't know what the woman she was looking for looked like. She scanned the people the coffee shop over Ruth's shoulder wondering if any of them were her.

"Well, I'm glad to see you here anyway. Don't worry about anything. Connie is gone for the day."

Cheryl's gaze hopped from face to face trying to figure out which one belonged to Sydney.

Ruth looked over her shoulder at the people sitting at the tables and then back at Cheryl. "I don't want to hold you up. Are you drinking anything?" She returned to her place behind the counter.

Cheryl stood holding a cup of coffee and looking at the tables before her. Four women sat alone, and any of them could've been Sydney. She was considering going up to each of them and asking if they were waiting for her when one of the women sitting at the table closest to her stood up. She was short woman in yoga capri pants and an oversized T-shirt. Her mousy brown hair was pulled up in a ponytail. "Cheryl?"

"Sydney?" Cheryl wondered how the woman knew it was her.

Sydney sighed with relief. "I'm glad it's you. You're the fourth person I've asked in the last few minutes. It was starting to get embarrassing."

Starting to get embarrassing? Cheryl thought. She would've been embarrassed to ask the first person. She took a seat across the table from Sydney. "Have you been here long?" Cheryl knew she wasn't late. She had made a point of being on time.

Sydney shook her head. "Only a few minutes. I tend to get places early."

They chatted a bit before getting to the reason they were meeting. Cheryl liked finding out about people. The whole time they talked she was looking for clues as to why Sydney was getting these calls too. She found out Sydney was a fitness instructor and was going to acupuncture school at night. Cheryl told her all about her work reading tarot cards. Sydney had lots of questions. People always had lots of questions when they found out what Cheryl did. As usual, she found herself telling a little too much, like how she wasn't allowed to read cards in the Starlight Café anymore.

"I'm surprised you feel comfortable enough to come back," Sydney said before taking a sip of her soy latte.

"I don't. This is me pushing the boundaries." Time was ticking away, and they both had places to go. "So, about these phone calls..."

Sydney put her cup down. She looked around and leaned in lowering her voice to speak. Her story was similar to Cheryl's. One day she walked into her house, and the phone was ringing, the landline. "I know you're thinking who has a landline anymore," Sydney said self-consciously. "My grandmother stayed with me for a while. I got it then because she didn't have a cell phone. I just never got around to getting rid of it when she left."

Cheryl nodded. "You don't have to explain it to me. I have one too."

"Yeah, but yours is for work."

"It doesn't matter," Cheryl said. "Go on with your story."

Sydney picked up where she left off. Her story was mostly the same as Cheryl's except for one part. "I came home from work the other day, and the phone was ringing," Sydney said. "I answered it, and this time there was silence on the other end. I said hello a few times and just when I was about to hang up the crackling sound started again. It didn't even scare me this time because I'd gotten so used to it. The crackling didn't last long before it dropped off into silence. Then a creaky male voice started talking. He apologized three times before he told me to call the Spirit Guides Network. He said that you could help."

"How?"

Sydney shrugged. "I don't know. He didn't tell me that."

Cheryl was kind of disappointed. She didn't know why she expected Sydney to know more than she already did. "Was that the last time you got a call?"

"No, last night I was asleep when the phone started ringing. I picked it up. It was all the same stuff, static and whining, and the voice asking for help."

Cheryl nodded knowingly.

"It was two o'clock in the morning. I checked when I answered the phone. Three minutes after two to be exact. When it first started, every time I got the phone call I couldn't sleep that night. I would have to go to a friend's house to spend the night, but I'm used to it now. I took the phone call and drifted right off again."

"When the voice told you to call me did it tell you anything else?"

Sydney sat back in her chair and looked up as she tried to remember. "The voice said I should call you. It gave me the number and told me what time to call. The voice said you could see him. He told me you would know what to do and you would know why he was calling me."

Cheryl shook her head.

"I'm sorry I don't know more. I wish I did." Sydney glanced up at the clock on the wall. "I have to go soon. I have a class to teach."

"I guess we're done here anyway," Cheryl said. "The voice mentioned me by name when he gave you my number?"

Sydney nodded. She finished the last sip of her latte. "Sure did."

"What did he mean when he said I could see him? How am I supposed to know what to do?"

"Beats me." Sydney wiped her mouth with a napkin and balled it up putting it in her cup. "He didn't give me any details."

Cheryl's eyes widened as she noticed a man in the back of the coffee shop. He seemed to have come out of the wall. His body was slightly transparent like all the other ghosts she'd seen since working with the Butlers at Adam's house. Cheryl wondered if he needed help. On one side of his narrow face the skin was white with blue veins rising out of the flesh and on the other side the skin puckered and oozed. His eyeball seemed to have melted down his face and his nose was missing its tip. He wandered casually between the tables with his hands in the pockets of his singed jeans. His white T-shirt, burned away on the right side, exposed the raw skin on his chest. His right arm was almost only bone. He seemed unaware of his deformities. He walked toward her confidently, his stride steady and slow. The horror of his appearance took her breath away. She hated to admit the way he looked scared her.

"Oh yeah, the voice wanted me to tell you to listen

more carefully. You aren't really listening. That's a mistake. You can't rely on your eyes for everything. You have to listen."

Cheryl cocked her head at Sydney. "What's that supposed to mean?" She kept the man in her sights.

Sydney shrugged. "You're supposed to know, not me."

"Why would they send a message to me through you? Who are you?" The man was only a foot from their table now. He finally looked at Cheryl, directly. His eyes were dark holes. He opened his mouth, and the same crackling sound from the phone calls poured out. The sound swept over the room drowning out every other noise in the busy café. Cheryl couldn't hear Sydney. She couldn't hear anything, but the deafening noise spilling from the man's mouth.

CHAPTER SIXTEEN

"STOP!" Cheryl clamped her hands over her ears and cried out. Terror surged through her. Her muscles tensed. The man reached out his hand as if he would grab her. Cheryl scooted back in her chair, the legs scraping on the tile floor. The chair tipped and almost fell over as the man reached for her. Cheryl clamped her eyes closed, preparing to feel him touch her but felt nothing. He seemed to pass through her and disintegrate like smoke. The crackling sound stopped suddenly making way for the normal buzz of the coffee shop.

"Are you okay?"

Cheryl opened her eyes to see Sydney standing next to her. Cheryl blinked a few times. "Yeah. I think so." She looked around the coffee shop. The ghost was nowhere to be seen.

Sydney reached down placing her hand and Cheryl's shoulder. "Are you sure? You gave me a real scare."

"Did you see or hear anything weird just then?"

Sydney shook her head.

Cheryl went to pick up her coffee cup and noticed her hands were shaking too badly. Afraid she would spill it she set it back on the saucer.

"Is there somebody I can call to come get you? I feel bad leaving you here like this, but I really do have to get to class." Sydney pulled her cell phone out of the canvas crossbody bag she wore over her shoulder.

"No." Cheryl shook her head. She couldn't think of anyone she would want Sydney to call. All this was so new, no one in her life knew about it, except Adam. She didn't want to call him. He was just a client, and she was trying to keep it that way. She'd already texted him to cancel the dinner he had tried to schedule. She just didn't feel comfortable going out with him even though he was nice, and if she was honest with herself, she thought he was good-looking. She liked his face, the way his eyes crinkled up the corners when he smiled. "I'll be fine. Get to your class."

Sydney tucked a stray hair behind her ear, looked toward the coffee shop door, and bit her lip. "Let me give you my number. Give me a call in about an hour just to let me know you're all right."

Cheryl agreed to do that. She had wanted to get Sydney's number anyway.

"Don't forget to call me," Sydney said before turning to leave.

"He told you I need to listen more, is that right?"

Sydney turned back around to answering over her

shoulder. "That's right."

"I was just checking. Have a good class." Cheryl waved.

What could that possibly mean? There must have been something in the calls she was missing, but what? She wondered if the ghost she'd just seen in the coffee shop was the same one who had kept calling them both. He must've been because she had seen a few ghosts since that day at Adam's house and this was the first one to open his mouth and only have that terrible static come out. What was she supposed to be listening for? She took a few deep breaths, trying to calm herself before picking up her coffee cup again. Her hands shook a little less this time. The caffeine was probably not the best for her right now, but the warm liquid going down her throat relaxed her. Her cell phone vibrated, clattering on the table for her attention. She was grateful to see Stephanie's name on the screen.

"Hey, Steph. How are you doing?"

"I'm on top of the world." Her voice was round and bright as a tangerine.

"You're in a good mood." Cheryl was grateful for that. "What's going on?"

"First of all, things are moving along really well for Damon and me. I'm practically living with him."

"That's great, but don't forget he's on the rebound."

"You keep reminding me of that. Can't you just let me have this moment?"

"You're my friend, I don't want you to get hurt." Cheryl scanned the coffee shop the whole time hoping the ghost didn't appear. Feeling like he might be behind her, she twisted around in her chair and noticed Connie standing behind the counter. She whipped back around and wondered if Connie had seen her.

"Everybody gets hurt eventually. If you don't put yourself out there, you won't find happiness."

"I guess you're right. You've been hurt so much though, I get protective sometimes." Stephanie was more than willing to put herself out there with guys. Often, she ended up getting rejected. Cheryl always told her it was because she was a bit too eager.

"I also wanted to know how that haunting you told me about was going."

"It's over."

"Because you got rid of the ghosts?"

"I think I got rid of them. We have to wait and see if they come back."

"You're kidding. How did you do that?"

Cheryl put her elbow on the table and rested her head in her hand, shaking her head.

"Are you still there?"

"Yeah," Cheryl said. "You have no idea what I've been going through."

"Only because you haven't told me. What's going on?"

"I can't even begin to explain, Stephanie." She thought about everything that had happened in the last few days. "The woman ghost ... her name is Miriam. She told me their story. A lot of what Betty told me was right."

"I'm so glad Betty could help. She's great," Stephanie said. "What's their story?"

Cheryl told Stephanie what Miriam had told her. "The craziest part was they were haunting Adam because he is

Charles' great-grandson—or is it two greats? I don't know. I'm too stressed to think about it."

"What's stressing you? You should be happy. You solved your first haunting."

Cheryl lowered her voice and cupped her hand around her mouth. She didn't want anyone else in the coffee shop to overhear what she was going to say next. "Ever since getting rid of Adam's ghosts, I've been seeing ghosts everywhere, and they all want me to help them. I'm in the Starlight Café ..."

"What are you doing there? I thought you were never going back." Stephanie was angrier about Cheryl's firing than Cheryl ever was.

"I had to meet someone. That's not the point of the story. A ghost who looked like he'd been burned to death walked right up to me and tried to touch me. I almost had a heart attack."

"What? That's insane. You mean you see ghosts all around, and they look like they did when they died or something?"

"Not all of them. This one did though."

"I would've peed my pants." Stephanie sounded as scared as Cheryl felt.

"I almost did."

"No wonder you're stressed."

Cheryl was glad she believed her and didn't assume she was crazy.

"At least you helped your client. You're braver than me." Stephanie laughed as she spoke. "I would've run out onto the street screaming if I saw a ghost."

"I did that the first time." If Cheryl had realized then what she would end up doing later, she would've been amazed. Thinking about it now amazed her. "You don't know how brave you are until you're put into a situation where bravery is required. Don't underestimate yourself."

"I'm pretty sure I'm not brave." Cheryl could hear someone speaking in the background. "I have to go," Stephanie said. "I'm at work. We need to get together soon though. I'll text you."

"Sounds good." Without the distraction of the phone call, Cheryl became aware of how afraid she felt. The tiny hairs in her arms stood on end, and she could hear every thud of her heart. She swung around in her chair to look around the coffee shop looking for the burnt ghost again. He was nowhere to be seen. Everyone around her seemed to be alive.

Connie came out from behind the counter and started walking toward her. Cheryl turned in her chair again to face the opposite wall. The last thing she wanted to do was talk to Connie.

"It's good to see you, Cheryl," Connie said, walking between the tables to get to her. "I'm glad you didn't let what happened stop you from coming here. You're always welcome, of course."

"Thanks. To be honest, I feel a bit weird about coming here. I wasn't sure I was welcome, and the whole misunderstanding we had was quite embarrassing. I liked doing readings here. I've always liked it here, but I guess that doesn't matter." Cheryl wanted to kick herself for saying too much. Why couldn't she ever stop talking?

"Of course it matters. You're welcome back here as long as you always pay for your drinks."

Embarrassed, Cheryl laughed, but Connie wasn't laughing. Noticing, Cheryl stopped laughing too. Her face fell. "I should go."

"Okay." Connie started to gather up the dirty cups and plates at the table near the window. "See you again soon." She walked back over to the counter, balancing the dishes in her hands.

Cheryl didn't finish her coffee. She couldn't stand the idea of staying there another minute. She walked past the counter as fast she as possible. When she stepped outside into the sun, her fear subsided. The day was bright and beautiful, and she was certain the ghost with the burn would not bother her out in the sunlight. She needed to talk to someone about what she'd seen, and the only person she could think of who might understand was Adam.

CHAPTER SEVENTEEN

ADAM stood in his living room holding his cell phone in his hand. Cheryl had gotten rid of the ghost. He'd felt their absence after she left, but his apartment still didn't feel right. The tight feeling in his chest persisted while he sat in the kitchen. Sometimes when he watched television, he'd notice a prickling feeling running up his neck and creeping over the top of his head.

The shower stopped turning on by itself and the doors and windows no longer flung themselves open at will, but there was something else wrong. He knew it. He'd thought about calling Cheryl several times to ask her if she could see anything, anyone else out of the ordinary in his home, but she'd canceled their dinner. She insisted he pay her online, which he did, but he still wanted to see her again. He longed to talk to her.

Every time he went to dial her number it was like his hand was paralyzed. He couldn't manage to call her. He couldn't imagine what he would say. He couldn't put his finger on what was wrong exactly, not like before.

Instead of calling her, he spent his free time cleaning his apartment. He hauled garbage bags bulging with stuff he should have thrown away long ago. He sorted through scraps of paper and unopened mail. He washed dishes until his hands were pruned, the skin so soft and wrinkled it could slough off. As he uncovered each area of his apartment, stripping away the debris of what the haunting had made his life, he expected the lump in his throat to disappear too. When it didn't, he'd move to the next room, the disappointment wedging itself in the thin muscle between his shoulder blades and the flesh at the base of his neck.

He hadn't expected her to call him, in a moment of desperation, her voice etched with panic. He didn't expect her to ask to see him, not since she'd gotten rid of the Butlers, not since she'd canceled dinner.

Cheryl didn't want to meet him at the Starlight Café. Instead, she wanted him to meet her at the juice and smoothie place that had opened a few blocks from his apartment. He wasn't a juice and smoothie kind of guy. He associated those places with men who did yoga and wore man buns.

Cheryl was sitting inside at one of the white tables drinking an unfortunately dark-green frothy drink. Adam made a beeline for her. "What's wrong?" he asked as he approached.

"Are you going to get a drink?"

He shook his head. The question surprised him. She had seemed so anxious on the phone he'd half expected her to break down as soon as she saw him. "Everything here is too healthy for me. I'd rather get a milkshake or something artery-clogging."

She didn't smile. She took a sip of her drink. Her face soured as she did.

"Whatever that witch's brew is you're drinking doesn't look very appetizing."

"It's good. It tastes like apples." She slid the cup across the table to him. "Try it."

"I'll pass. They don't have beer here, do they?"

That time she did laugh, and her face relaxed. "I doubt it."

Adam pulled out the chair across from her and sat down. "You sounded so upset when you called. What's wrong?"

"I'm losing my mind. I thought you might be the only person who would understand."

"Because I'm crazy?"

She shook her head. "No, but because when you were being haunted, you thought you were crazy too, didn't you?"

He nodded slowly. He was still losing his mind, but he didn't want to tell her that now. They were there because of her. She needed him for a change.

"Ever since that day, I can see them all around." She rubbed the back of her neck and looked around the room. Dark circles marked the space beneath her eyes, and her whole body seemed to sag with fatigue.

"Who? The Butlers?"

"Other ones like them. They are everywhere and when they figure out I can see them they all want something from me.

He watched her carefully. Her movements were sluggish, her words slow and precise.

"You mean ghosts?" he asked. Before he was being haunted himself, he'd never even considered the possibility of ghosts walking among the living, but that had all changed. He often wondered if there were lots of them, everywhere like Cheryl said. He wondered why they didn't always try to communicate with the living.

Suddenly she seemed more alert. She pushed herself up straight in her chair, her eyes trained on something just over his head. "We should go." She stood up quickly and picked her cup up from the table.

Adam followed her as she walked at a fast clip out of the shop. "Was there one in there just then?"

"There were four, but one of them started to approach us. I want to help them, I do. I helped one on the way back from your place."

"How'd you do that?"

She took a sip of her drink. "I told his mother and sister that his death wasn't their fault, and that he loved them and knew they had only wanted the best for him."

"That's all."

She nodded. "That's all he wanted. I think he needed to make sure they were going to be all right before he could move on." Suddenly she stopped walking, and when Adam looked around he realized they were in front of his building. "Can I come up?" She looked at the door and back at him.

"Of course."

She stood in the middle of the living room and looked around like she never been there before.

"Are you okay?" Adam asked. He kicked off his flip-flops by the door. "Do you want anything? Some water?"

She shook her head absent-mindedly. "You cleaned. It looks good in here."

"It was a lot of work, but well worth it. I hated living in that mess. I don't even know how it got that bad in the first place." Adam leaned against the door frame admiring his work. It was good to see the floor. He'd almost forgotten what color the carpet was. He'd even managed to hang up all the black-and-white photos he'd had framed from his trip around Asia when he was in college. "Can I get you something to drink?" he asked again as he walked across the living room to the kitchen. When she didn't answer again he turned to look at her. The muscles in her face tensed like she was focusing on something. She wore that face whenever she was in his house. Focus was like a plaster mask on her. He liked her face better when it was soft and relaxed, when she was smiling or laughing. He'd seen her looking that way many times in the café. Her brown skin radiated in the sunlight drawing his eyes to her automatically. "How come it doesn't feel quite right in here? They should be gone. It should be different, but I'm still getting that tightness in my chest." She looked at him as if realizing he was in the room with her for the first time.

Caught in her gaze, he froze. "I don't know, but sometimes I feel it too. It's not the same as when they were here, though. The feeling is different somehow."

He hadn't finished talking when she brushed past him

walking into the kitchen. She walked up to the table and rested her hand on the back of the same chair she'd sat on last time she was there. She bit her lip and thought for a moment. "I don't get it." She turned her head to look at him again.

"All of the weird stuff has stopped, but there's still something that's not quite right." He watched her turn in a circle in the room. "What do you think it is?"

She didn't answer. She rushed through the living room and into his bedrooms. Adam followed her as she flung open the closet doors.

"What are you doing?" he asked, following on her heels. She looked behind doors and open dresser drawers. "Are you looking for them?"

She didn't answer. This woman who could do so much talking had suddenly decided to stop using her voice. She rushed into his spare bedroom and looked under the bed. Then opened the closet. Adam hadn't gotten around to cleaning that out yet, and it was packed full of boxes. A few of them nearly tumbled out before she before she closed the closet door, forcing it shut with a thud.

Adam reached out and took hold of her arm. "Why are you going through my stuff?"

Her eyes widened with a panic that sent a chill through Adam. In all his years of living, no one had ever looked at him like that. They both froze for a moment, and it was as if time stood still. "I'm sorry," he finally said, letting go of her.

Her breath was ragged and shallow. She rubbed the place on her arm where he'd grabbed her all the while not taking her eyes off him.

"Did I hurt you?" He didn't know how he could've. He'd barely held on to her at all, but there was clearly something wrong.

She continued looking at him and rubbing her arm. Her gaze thick with betrayal. Her body hunched.

"I'm sorry." He dared not try to touch her again. "You were making me nervous."

She leaned forward, putting her hands on her knees, and looking at the ground.

"Are you okay?"

She nodded. "Yes." Her voice sounded far away.

"What were you looking for?"

Her breathing slowing, she eased herself upright and looked up at him. Her eyes no longer burning with fear. "I don't know. I guess I was looking for the Butlers."

"And you thought you'd find them in my dresser drawers?"

"I don't know what I thought." As if realizing where she was suddenly, she hurried out of the bedroom into the living room. "I'm sorry. I didn't mean to violate your privacy." She picked her bag up from the sofa. "Your place looks nice. I'm glad you cleaned it up."

"Thanks," he said. "You're leaving? I thought we were going to try to figure out what was going on with you." Adam studied her.

She moved cautiously, like she was trying to navigate the minefield. She practically tiptoed to the door.

"Cheryl, don't leave." Adam hurried past her, putting himself between her and the door.

She stopped. Her wounded eyes held on to his. "I have to go. I can't explain, but I'll call you." Looking at the floor, she rubbed the back of her neck.

"You're making me nervous. Are you sure you're all right?"

She sighed and shifted her weight. "I don't know. My sanity seems to be unraveling. I've been getting these weird phone calls on my landline."

"Who has a landline anymore?"

She looked up at him, her forehead creased. "It's for work."

"I'm sorry. Go ahead."

"Anyway, I've been getting these calls that are all crackling sounds and then a kid begging for me to help him. They're creepy, and I kept thinking they must be a prank, but today I think I saw the ghost who has been making them at the Starlight Café."

"I thought you weren't going there anymore." He knew it wasn't the point but wondered why she was there.

"This ghost wasn't like the other ones. The ghosts I've seen have all seemed lost. This one wasn't lost. He was looking for me."

He tried to imagine seeing a ghost himself. He didn't know if it would have been better or worse than what he'd already experienced with the Butlers. "What did he do?"

"Nothing really. I guess he kind of yelled at me."

"Kind of yelled at you?" He wasn't sure what that meant.

"I get the feeling he couldn't do anything to me even though he wanted to. Maybe all they can really do is scare us." She looked into his eyes as if she wanted him to say something reassuring. He wasn't sure what could be reassuring in this situation.

"I was hoping you could help me figure all this out. It's bigger than just the Butlers and what's been going on in your apartment. Something else is happening, and we have to find out what."

He wasn't expecting this. She was thinking of him as a partner and not just a client. Adam stepped to the side to let her go by him. "Does that mean you'll have dinner with me?" He had to ask.

She smiled. "How about a lunch meeting?"

"Don't try to make it business. I'll have lunch with you, but I want to relax."

"It's hard to relax when you see ghosts all around you. We can have a relaxing lunch to celebrate solving this." She reached out and pulled the door open. She brushed past him to get out into the hall.

"I can take you home."

She stood with one foot out of his apartment and one foot in, her hand on the door. She looked down the stairs that led to the street and then back over at him. "That would be nice," she said.

Chapter Eighteen

THEY drove to Cheryl's house in silence. The seatbelt hugged Cheryl uncomfortably around the chest. She'd accepted the ride because she knew she had no reason to be afraid of Adam, but when he grabbed her arm, his touch brought with it a flood of memories.

"That's it. There on the right." Cheryl pointed through the windshield to the stucco building she called home. Adam pulled his white SUV into a parking space in front of it and stopped. "Thanks for the ride." There was no way he would understand how much she meant that. Even as she rode in his SUV, she could see the spirits on the street. One sat on the curb just outside of her door in a dark gray suit, balancing a black fedora on his knees. He looked straight ahead seeming oblivious to the car that had just parked in front of him. He looked so sad that Cheryl considered going over to help him when she got out of the car, but she was too tired for that.

"I didn't mean to scare you back there. I shouldn't have grabbed you like that." He looked at her with his gray-blue eyes. Cheryl found herself wondering what he might be thinking. She wondered if the world looked different to him than they did to her own dark brown eyes.

"I shouldn't have been going through your stuff. I'm sorry about that. I don't know what I was doing." She opened the car door.

"We're both sorry then."

She nodded slowly. "I felt like there was still a ghost there—not the Butlers, but someone else. I was just trying to figure out who it was and where they were hiding."

He looked out the windshield. Cheryl found herself wishing he could see what she saw, a world pulsing with the living and the dead. "Did you see anyone?"

Cheryl shook her head. "I wish I had, but I only felt it."

She was beginning to regain her equilibrium. Thinking of how she reacted when Adam grabbed her arm made her flush with embarrassment. She longed to go back in time and change what had happened to her, so she wouldn't react like that. "I'm doing some readings at a new age store tonight at seven. They're having a special event, and I know one of the other psychics who will be there. I think I'll ask her if she has any suggestions."

"That would be good." He looked over at her again.

Cheryl knew she should get out of the car but didn't. She just sat there looking out the window watching the spirit sitting on the curb. The thought of going into her own house made her blood run cold. She had to do it now. She jumped out of the SUV. "Thanks again for the ride."

"I'll call you," he said.

"Okay." She shut the car door. She had to walk close to the spirit on the curb to get into her building. She fought her instinct to make a wide circle around him because she knew doing so would only let on she could see him. That was the last thing she wanted, so she walked within inches of where he sat. His black suit looked faded in the dusky light. Cheryl didn't want to look directly at him. When she got to the glass doors of her building, Adam was still sitting in his SUV watching her. She turned around to wave at him, and when she did, the ghost turned and looked at her too, as if realizing for the first time he wasn't on the street alone. Cheryl hurried into her building to avoid looking into his vacant eyes. As she rushed up the stairs, she expected him to follow her. He didn't, but she didn't feel relief until she was in her apartment.

Beau greeted her with a creaky meow, and she scooped him up into her arms. "Did anything weird happen while I was gone?" she asked him, surveying the apartment to see if anything was out of place. She only had a few minutes to relax and snuggle with Beau on the couch before she'd have to get ready for her reading that night. Holding Beau close to her chest, she flopped back onto the sofa. It was much too big for her tiny apartment. She'd known that when she'd moved in but couldn't afford the luxury of buying new furniture back then. She still couldn't. She closed her eyes and wondered if there would ever be a time when her finances wouldn't be such a struggle.

Cheryl closed her eyes. She needed a few minutes of rest, but every time she closed her eyes she could see the ghost with the burns from the Starlight Café in her mind.

Her eyes flew open to see Beau curled up sleeping on her lap. His fur was a swirl of black and gray. Sleepily, he opened his green eyes and gave her a few slow blinks before closing them again. He was calm, so Cheryl had no reason to be freaking out. That's what she kept telling herself as her heartbeat sped and her breathing became more and more frantic. She swallowed hard, a lump forming in her throat.

"What's happening?" she asked no one. Maybe she was having a heart attack or just a panic attack.

She sat up straight, trying to take a deep breath, but couldn't. Maybe this was a dream, and she was still sleeping. The pain radiating across her chest told her otherwise. She leaned over, her arm extended to reach the telephone on the end table. Annoyed, Beau leaped from her lap and scurried into the bedroom. Just as her fingertips touched the phone, it started to ring, sharp and violent. It was much more distressful than any ring she had ever heard before.

Cheryl froze. Her ears tuned in to the sound, and she tried to figure out what she should do next. She didn't have to think long because the ring stopped as suddenly as it started. Silence ripped through the house. It was quieter than normal, no traffic sounds outside, no sound from the refrigerator in the kitchen, Cheryl couldn't even hear her own heartbeat. For a moment, Cheryl thought she might be dead. Leaning forward, she tried to stand up but couldn't. Her legs were like weights anchoring her to the sofa. No matter how hard she strained, she couldn't stand. Panicked, her eyes searched the room. Fear ravaged her.

She saw his hand first. One by one his fingers curled around the doorframe that led from the hallway to the living room. The skin was so white and thin it did nothing to hide the veins clearly visible beneath. The fingers drummed the wall a few times before gripping hard like they were pulling him from the other side. He appeared slowly, straining to get himself into the doorway. It was the same ghost from the coffee shop, the same one who had been haunting her thoughts. His shoulders sloped unnaturally. His rib cage pushed through the burnt skin of his chest like it was trying to escape his body. His pants drooped lazily around his hipbones. He lurched forward.

Cheryl opened her mouth to scream, but nothing came out. She felt like a rope was tied around her vocal cords. Her muscles strained as she tried to move. It was useless. She could only watch him stumbling toward her, her breath ragged, her chest thumping in the impossible silence of this place. When he reached her, he reached out his hand like he had before. His hand got closer and closer to her head. She could see a mole, the color of night, on the palm of his hand where it met the wrist. His index finger reached her forehead, and this time it made physical contact, cold and hard, like death being pressed into her. An image flashed in her head of a young girl wearing a light blue nightgown, her blonde hair in two messy pigtails. The girl's face twisted with fear as she clung to a woman with dusty, red hair. Cheryl couldn't push the image out of her head. He was holding it in her brain, making her see it. She could only surrender to it. When she thought she might be on the edge of death, her breathing shallow, her heart beating so quickly it might burst, he vanished. The molecules that made him scampered off in every direction like a fog chased away by the morning light.

Cheryl took deep gulping breaths like she was coming up to the surface for air. Her head fell back. Her back arched. Her forehead tingled in the spot where he had touched her head. She rubbed the place with her hand and tears began to flow from her eyes making salty trails down her face. She tried to stand but was so weak she nearly collapsed to the floor. She returned to the couch, her body convulsing with frightened sobs. She didn't know what to do. She could call Adam again, but what could he do? She thought about calling Stephanie because she needed to hear someone's voice. She needed to listen to something familiar to shake off this feeling.

She took her cell phone from her purse and began to call Stephanie. Before the phone rang, she hung up. She remembered she was supposed to call Sydney to let her know she was all right. Of all the people she knew, Sydney and Adam were the ones that were most likely to understand what was happening to her. She had just talked to Adam and didn't want to bother him again, so she called Sydney.

"Hello?" Her voice was deeper and harsher than before.

"Sydney?" Cheryl said.

"Yeah."

"This is Cheryl, the tarot card reader." She didn't know why but for some reason Cheryl thought Sydney might not recognize her name. "You told me to call you, to tell you I was okay."

"Cheryl," her voice lightened. "Are you doing any

better? You seemed pretty shaken up at the café."

"I was. I saw something." The idea of explaining this to a stranger was hard. Cheryl had a difficult enough time explaining it to Stephanie, her closest friend, and then to Adam. She'd only met Sydney once. Even though they have the same problem the strange phone calls, she didn't know how Sydney felt about ghosts. "I can see ghosts. It's only been happening for the last couple days. It's really weird, and I know I probably sound like a lunatic, but that's it. I see dead people like the kid from The Sixth Sense." Cheryl waved her hands around as she spoke.

"Okay?"

"I know it sounds crazy, but it's true." Cheryl listened. She wanted Sydney to say something before she went on. She wanted her to believe her.

"My grandmother used to see spirits. She was Ukrainian and could hardly speak a lick of English, but she used to cast spells and hexes. Sometimes she would look like she was having a seizure and start speaking in a completely different voice. I didn't want to believe it. As a child, it terrified me, but as I got older, I learned to accept it. She's gone now, but I like to think her spirit is still with me."

Cheryl exhaled, and the tension drained from her muscles. "So, you believe me?"

"I don't know. You could be lying to me, but when I saw you at the café you had that look my grandmother used to get sometimes, and with all the crazy stuff that's been going on with me, anything is possible."

"I've been learning that recently too." Cheryl thought

about all the things that had happened to her in the past couple of weeks. When she first talked to Adam, she had no idea her life would never be the same. "You're right. I saw a ghost in the café. I think it's the one that's been calling us because when it opened its mouth only the crackling sound I hear on the phone came out."

"What does he want from us?"

"I don't know. He hasn't told me yet."

"Have you gotten any more calls?" Sydney asked.

"No. He doesn't have to call if he can just show up in person." How Cheryl longed for the days of the creepy phone calls. It was much less frightening than seeing him.

"I got a call as soon as I got home." Sydney said it so calmly that anyone listing and would've thought she had gotten a call from a telemarketer.

"Did he say anything different?" Cheryl needed clues.

"Yeah. The childish voice said it was almost too late and you needed to listen." The sentence rose up at the end of the Sydney were asking a question even though she was not.

"What does that mean?" Cheryl wondered why the ghost had said everything in riddles. She wanted her life to be more straightforward than this.

"I was hoping you would know."

Cheryl's head hurt. "Somebody should make some kind of ghost to English dictionary or something, I swear. Why do they have to make it so hard? Aren't they the ones suffering? Don't they need us to help them get to wherever they're going? I don't understand why it has to be so difficult. Is it because they're bored?"

Sydney laughed. "Now you mention it, I have no idea why they have to make it so hard. I wonder if my grandmother knew."

"If your grandmother was still hanging out with you I could ask her."

"I like to think that she is." Sydney's voice had a wistful faraway sound.

Cheryl hadn't seen Sydney's grandmother anywhere around her, but that didn't mean she wasn't there. "It's good to have someone on the other side looking out for you. Believe me, right now I wish I had that." Cheryl imagined the ghost of her great-grandfather who was a particularly tough man beating up the burned ghost. She had no idea if that was even possible or justified. So far, the ghost had done nothing more than scare her, and she wondered if he was even doing that intentionally.

It was good talking to Sydney. It made Cheryl feel a little less crazy. She decided not to tell her about the most recent visit from the ghost. She felt it might freak Sydney out too much. It had freaked her out, a lot. She didn't want to relive it, not now she needed to come down, so she could be at her best at the reading tonight.

They talked a bit more about things other than ghosts which was good because Cheryl needed to focus on something else. She insisted they would remain friends after this ordeal was over.

Cheryl hurried down the stairs and out the front door of her building, the strap of her purse falling from her shoulder. She stopped to hike it back up and continued. She hadn't even noticed his SUV as she turned to walk up the sidewalk. He honked his horn, and she jumped.

The window glided down. "I thought I'd give you a lift."

"You don't have to do that." The last thing she ever wanted to do was inconvenience anyone.

Adam leaned over and opened the passenger's side door. "Get in."

The night air was fresh. It was the type of evening that always put Cheryl in a good mood, even after being touched on the forehead by an incredibly creepy ghost. She felt like she could float away into the night. She almost told him "no" again because some quiet time in her car seemed appealing at the moment. Then she looked down the sidewalk and noticed two ghosts standing near her car. "Okay," she said as she climbed into his car. "You can just drop me off. I'll get an Uber home or something."

"Why would I do that? I'll stay. You can think of me as your personal escort."

"I'm pretty sure it's not your scene." She pulled the door closed.

"How do you figure that? After what's happened to me, it's all my scene. I'll hang out. Maybe I can find out what else we need to do to get all this to stop." He pulled away from the curb.

"That would be good." Cheryl leaned back in the passenger seat. She wouldn't tell him about the ghost in her apartment, not yet. She'd save that story for later. She needed to ground herself and prepare for the work she was about to do.

CHAPTER NINETEEN

THERE was a time when Adam would've never set foot in one of these shops, but since the haunting started, he'd frequented them. He had been to this particular store before with its glass displays of crystals and shelves filled with books about angels in spirit and touching the divine. A few years ago, he would've been the first to tell you all this was a ridiculous waste of time. There was no afterlife. There were no spirits, ghosts, or hauntings. The body was a machine run by a complicated web of neurons. Adam had always assumed when he died, he would cease to exist. Wasn't that what was supposed to happen?

He hadn't grown up with religion and never had the time to think about such things. He liked concrete explanations for life. He liked research and studies backed by science.

His life had changed so much. Here he was, standing in a new age bookstore, surrounded by people with names like Rainbow and Sunshine talking about their spirit guides. He was spending time with a tarot card reader who could see ghosts and who was one of the most beautiful women he had ever seen. He couldn't believe he'd seen her several times a week at the café, and though he noticed her, he hadn't really noticed. The way she bit her lip when she was thinking, the hollow at the base of her neck where her collarbones met, the way she smelled like Christmastime even in March, all of her intrigued him.

Adam stood in the corner and watched her work. She spoke to a man whose thin graying hair hung unevenly around his shoulders. A patch of shiny scalp was visible at the back of his head. He leaned forward and listened to Cheryl talk, captivated. How could he not be? Adam had become captivated too.

"That's a good book," a raspy voice said to him.

Adam hadn't noticed the slender silver-haired woman standing next to him. She wore a teal and purple shawl over her dark gray dress. "To be honest, I was just holding it, so I didn't stand out."

She grinned. "It didn't work."

He went to put the book back on the shelf, but before he could, she took it from him. "I've read it several times."

Adam nodded his head. "Several times?"

She nodded too and opened the book to a page in the middle and looked at it for a few moments. "It talks about the spirits that live among us. Did you know we are surrounded by our ancestors all the time?" she looked up at him with piercing emerald eyes.

"I've been learning that recently."

"Really? How?"

He looked over at Cheryl again before returning his

gaze to the woman.

"You're a friend of Cheryl?"

"Yes. Well." Suddenly he found himself wondering if they were friends. "I was a client. She did some work for me." He looked around and lowered his voice. "My apartment was haunted."

She took hold of his arm. "You don't have to whisper. That kind of thing doesn't have to be a secret, not in a place like this."

"Point taken." Adam looked at the book in her hand. "Since you've read that book several times maybe you could teach me a few things about hauntings. Cheryl hadn't dealt with ghosts before. She kept telling me she was in over her head, but she did a great job. I mean they are gone ... At least we thought they were gone, but now we think they might be back."

She cocked her head at him. "Why do you think they're back?"

"It's hard to explain. The apartment doesn't feel right."

"How long have these spirits been haunting you?"

It had been going on so long Adam was starting to feel like they had always been with him even though that wasn't the case. "For almost a year."

"Did you live in the same apartment that whole time?" Her stare was so intense he wanted to turn away.

He cleared his throat and looked over at Cheryl again. She'd finished up with her client and was gathering the cards on her table into a stack as someone else sat down for a reading. "No, I moved after I realized the other place I was living in was haunted. I didn't realize the ghosts were haunting me and not the house."

Her eyes widened as if she'd seen something important. "Ever since you've lived in that apartment it's been haunted. Is that what you're telling me?"

"I guess so."

She nodded knowingly. She didn't have to tell Adam what she was thinking because he already knew.

"I feel strange because I've never known what the apartment feels like when it isn't haunted. That uncomfortable feeling I get in my chest now isn't because there are more ghosts there, but because I'm alone in the apartment for the first time since I've lived there."

"Bingo," she said, pointing at him. "I've never been to your apartment, so I could be wrong. What did Cheryl say?"

"She thought it didn't feel right either. Last time she was there she ran around looking for ghosts."

The woman pressed her thin lips together in a tight line that nearly made them disappear. Her forehead furrowed. "Interesting, because Cheryl has good instincts. If she thinks there is another spirit there, she could be right."

"You've worked with her before?"

The woman cleared her throat. "The psychic community here is small. We all know each other."

"Oh. I didn't realize you were a psychic. What kind of work do you do?" Adam had changed in the past year. Previously, he didn't even know psychics did different types of work. To him, a psychic was a psychic. Now he knew they read palms or auras or cards. There were probably a million other things they did he didn't know about yet.

"I do a little bit of everything. The tool I use depends

on the client and what makes them feel comfortable." She glanced over at Cheryl who had been busy all night. "She's got good instincts, but she doesn't trust herself, and she doesn't charge enough. She could be an excellent psychic if she got that part of things together." There was pity in her eyes. "I understand. I was young once too. I was always confident in my abilities, but there are other things I wasn't confident about. I know what it's like to doubt yourself. I also know what it's like to stop doubting yourself, and I wish Cheryl would learn to stop. She has so much potential."

Adam didn't know how to judge people's abilities. "Cheryl helped me. I worked with a lot of people before her, and she was the only one who helped." Adam felt a certain amount of pride when he realized the woman respected Cheryl's abilities, which was funny, because he had done nothing that made her psychic. "Did she tell you what happened to her after she helped me with my haunting?"

The woman raised an eyebrow at him. "Before she started doing the readings, she said she wanted to talk to me for a minute, but she hasn't told me anything yet. Fill me in."

Adam looked over at Cheryl again and then shook his head. "I should probably let her tell you. We're not close enough for me to interfere like that."

"You could've fooled me." She smirked. "I see the way you've been watching her all night. It doesn't take a psychic to see you've got a thing for her."

Adam felt his face flush. "It's not like that at all."

"Of course not." The woman looked down at the book

in her hand and then back at Adam's face. "I'm so rude. I forgot to introduce myself. I'm Day." She extended her small hand toward him.

"Day? Like a day of the week?"

"That's right. My mother liked calendars." She laughed.

"She could've named you June."

Day smiled, and her face crinkled. "I'm lucky. She could've named me Month or Week. At least Day sounds nice."

"You've got a point. I'm Adam." He took her hand in his and shook it. Her palms were warm and her fingers bony.

"Nice to meet you." She took her hand away and ruffled through the book. "Now that we have had a formal introduction would you like to know what I think you should do to make sure your ghost is gone?"

He nodded enthusiastically. "If you could tell me anything that would help that would be amazing."

"I assume you cleared the house already with sage."

"Ages ago when all this first started I had someone do that." He remembered the jolly woman with short green hair who had walked around his house burning a bundle of sage and saying a prayer in a language he didn't understand. Adam remembered thinking she was far too happy to chase away any spirits. She'd even broken into a fit of random laughter at one point that made him doubt her sanity. "It didn't work."

"Did you hire someone to do that for you?"

"Yeah. I think her name was a Rain Storm." Saying the name aloud made Adam laugh. He didn't know what had possessed him to hire the woman. He was so desperate he didn't notice her incompetence.

"No wonder." Day reached out and touched Adam's forearm. "That woman is a mess. I wouldn't hire her to make a sandwich yet alone clear my house of bad spirits. Smudge the apartment again. This time get Cheryl to do it for you. Then see how you feel. When done properly that should be enough to finish off the work Cheryl has already done. If it doesn't work you'll have to try something else, rice maybe."

"Rice?"

"You can leave a trail of rice around your house to lure the ghosts outside," she said it like it was perfectly logical, but it didn't make sense to Adam at all.

"Why would rice lure ghosts out?"

"They like to count," she said, and he found himself doubting every bit of the conversation they'd just had. It was funny how perceptions could switch so quickly. "I see the way you're looking at me."

He shifted uncomfortably. "What do you mean?"

"I'm not crazy. I'm telling you an important fact that will serve you in the future. All you have to do is try it to see if it works. Putting some raw rice around your house won't hurt anything."

"It will be hard because I live in an apartment."

"Put it around your building then." She had a self-satisfied smile on her face that showed she thought she was cleverer than she was.

"Did you learn that from that book?" He glanced down at the book in her hand.

"No. I learned from a Japanese friend. I had a client do it once, and it worked. The solutions in this book are more complicated, but sometimes you need something simple to get the job done. There's power in simplicity."

He shrugged. "I guess it's worth a try. It won't hurt."

Distracted by a tray of pinwheel sandwiches someone had placed on a table at the far side of the room, she said, "Try it and let me know how it goes." She drifted away from him as quickly as she had approached him.

If she were one of the best in the area, it was no wonder Adam had spent so much time and money trying to get rid of his ghosts. At the beginning of the conversation, he had assumed she knew what she was talking about. Maybe it was something about the gray hair and the way she carried herself that made him assume she had experience with these things. She probably never experienced anything as intense as he and Cheryl had experienced these past few days. How could she know how to solve a problem she never had? Why should she care? No wonder he couldn't get help before. No wonder the people Cheryl asked couldn't give her advice. If that's what they would have to work with, it was obvious they would have to figure this out on their own. The rice was worth a try though. She was right it wouldn't hurt.

CHAPTER TWENTY

"I had a little chat with your friend over there." Day nodded to Adam who was standing at the far side of the bookstore talking to a short blonde in a long, gauzy skirt.

Cheryl packed her supplies into her large sack-like handbag. "Adam? He's nice, isn't he?" Cheryl looked over at him leaning against the end of a bookshelf as he chatted. He was charming, especially now she had gotten to know him.

"He certainly does like you. He couldn't take his eyes off you the whole time he was talking to me."

"Seriously?" Adam was nice and not bad looking, but Cheryl was trying not to think of him romantically. He was a client, and right now they were involved in solving a problem. She didn't have enough time to think about much else, and since her last experience, the idea of being in a relationship was about as attractive as slamming her head against the wall repeatedly.

"His eyes light up when he talks about you. You can't tell me you haven't noticed."

Now that Day mentioned it, Cheryl might've noticed. He had told her he didn't want to stop seeing her. She'd convinced herself the dinner date he'd tried to arrange was to talk about the haunting, but inside she knew otherwise. "He's a client. He's just happy because I've been able to help them."

"About that," Day said. "Adam told me about the ghost. I gave him some advice about what to do to make sure they're out of his place. You know, the typical stuff: sage, putting rice around the building."

Cheryl furrowed her brow.

"You're looking at me the way he did. These things are common because they work. He seems to think his ghosts are still lurking around. If that's the case, something like burning sage will help push the last of them out, even if it didn't work before when they had a stronger hold on the place." Her words were so authoritative. She did have a lot more experience than Cheryl. Cheryl had gone to her for advice in the past, but this advice felt too simple.

"He tried all that before, and it didn't work."

Day let out an exasperated sigh. "Sometimes you just don't have enough faith. Give it a try and believe it. Do it with conviction. Sure, he's had someone smudge the house before, but he hasn't had you do it, has he?"

"You're right I didn't smudge the house. I didn't do it because it had already been done. It seemed like his problem was more complicated than I could deal with. I wasn't going to take his case, but he insisted."

"That's because he likes you." Day reached over and gave Cheryl's arm a squeeze.

This was getting old. "This is off the subject, but ever since doing the work at Adam's house something strange has been happening to me." Cheryl looked around to make sure no one else was paying attention to what she said next. "I've been seeing spirits. They're all around us, and they want me to help them. There are some here tonight."

Day looked around the room as if she would be able to see them too. "Where?"

"Over there, and over there, and over there." Cheryl pointed around the room as she talked. She leaned in and whispered in Day's ear. "There's one right behind you. He's been following you around all evening." The spirit was a man in his early 40s wearing a pair of denim shorts and a T-shirt with the year 1979 written in white across the chest. He wore his shoulder-length blond hair in a ponytail at the nape of his neck. Every time Cheryl made eye contact with him he would nod his head and smile.

Day turned around to get a good look behind her. "I don't see anyone. What does he look like?"

Cheryl described the man in detail which seemed to make him very happy. He swayed back and forth almost like he was doing a little bit of a dance.

As she spoke, Day's eyes began to swell with tears. "Eddie?" she whispered.

"Do you know him?" Cheryl looked at the man again, and he nodded. Suddenly it was as if he were talking, but his mouth was not moving. His words filled up Cheryl's mind. "He wants you to know you are the love of his life, and he's sorry it had to end so soon."

Day turned to look behind her again and then back at

Cheryl. She reached out to grab Cheryl's arm again, this time gripping it tightly like she was holding on for dear life. "Eddie is here?"

"Yes."

Day's intense emotional reaction threw Cheryl off balance. Her whole world was out of kilter. Day had always known so much more than her. She had been her bedrock when she doubted her own abilities, and here she was seeing something Day couldn't see.

"He wants to know if you remember the time you went on that rafting trip in the Grand Canyon."

Day nodded. "Of course I remember." Her voice was hoarse.

"He wants you to know it was one of the best times of his life and he meant what he said. He wants you to know he's been watching you and you've come a long way. He's happy about who you've become, and he regrets not being able to be here with you."

Day let go of Cheryl's arm. She turned around, tears flowing down her face. "It was the best time of my life too. I miss you so much. I never stopped thinking about you." Her voice quivered, and she took a step forward. For a moment Cheryl was afraid she might collapse on to the floor. "What's he saying now?"

"He says it's time for you both to move on."

"I don't know if I can." Day turned her head, so she could see Cheryl again. She wiped the tears from her eyes. Her face panicked.

"He says you can. He says you're strong and you're magic. You can move on from anything. He says he loves you, but he has to go now."

"I love you too." Eddie had already vanished before she'd even spoken the words. She reached out her hand like she was expecting to grab on to something, but there was only air in front of her. Day turned back around to face Cheryl, her face red and wet from crying. She'd always been so reserved that seeing her like this unnerved Cheryl. She stepped forward and gave Cheryl a long hug. "Thank you," she said. "Thank you." When she finally released Cheryl, she reached into her purse and pulled out a tissue to wipe her eyes. Once she had composed herself, she said, "That was amazing."

Cheryl didn't know what to say. "I only told you what he wanted to tell you himself but couldn't."

"I think you've found your calling in this world. You need to put the tarot cards away and start concentrating on that." When she said that, she pointed into the air at nothing in particular.

"I'm not even sure what that is." Cheryl couldn't imagine herself doing anything but tarot.

Day grabbed both of her shoulders and gave her little shake. "You commune with the dead. Don't you know how valuable that is? Don't you realize the good you could do? Look what you've done for me just now." Cheryl looked at her blankly, and Day dropped her arms to her sides. "You don't understand what you have."

"I don't think you understand. What I have has been tearing my life apart. I feel like I'm losing my mind. You haven't even heard the worst of it." Cheryl scanned the room to see if the ghost with the burn was there. Ever since he'd touched her head, she felt like he was watching her. She felt like he could show up at any moment.

"That's because it's new. Once you get used to it, once you learn how to use it, it won't be the same."

Just then, Cheryl felt two hands on her shoulders from behind. She jumped and turned her head to see Stephanie. "I like this place. It has a nice vibe, and all the books are interesting."

"I didn't know you were coming," Cheryl said. "Day, this is my friend Stephanie."

"I'm pretty sure we've met before."

Stephanie nodded. "I think we did."

Day was not her normal self. She stood looking blankly in Stephanie's direction for a few moments. "I'm sorry. I'm a bit ..." She dapped her eyes with a tissue. "I should get going. I'll let you and your friend catch up." She stood there for a moment like she wasn't sure what to do.

"Are you going to be okay?" Cheryl asked. She couldn't blame Day for being shaken by their previous conversation.

"I'm fine. Just fine." Day turned her attention back to Stephanie. "It was good seeing you again."

"You too," Stephanie said. Stephanie turned around and latched her arm around the arm of a tall brown-skinned man standing behind her. "Cheryl, I want you to meet Damon." She turned to Damon. "Cheryl is like one of my closest friends."

Hearing that pleased Cheryl because sometimes she wondered if their friendship was as important to Stephanie as it was to her. "Damon, I'm so glad to meet you. I've heard so much about you." Cheryl never understood the big deal

Stephanie made of him until now. He was very good-looking with strong features and close-cut dark hair. There was an intensity in his deep brown eyes that sent a little chill through Cheryl.

"I've heard a lot about you too," he said. "I wanted to get a reading from you today, but you were so busy."

"Damon has visions." Stephanie's words flitted over the noise of the crowd.

"They're just dreams." The way his face tensed when he said that let Cheryl know they were more than just dreams.

"Well, I would be happy to give you reading sometime." Stephanie seemed to go all gooey every time she looked at him. That made Cheryl nervous because she noticed he didn't look at her the same way. The reserve in his gaze confirmed her fears this relationship was just a rebound for him and Stephanie was not prepared to deal with that. She couldn't tell Stephanie what to do. She was always so hardheaded.

Cheryl caught Adam's eye at the back corner of the room. He finished his conversation with the blonde and was heading their way.

Noticing Cheryl was smiling at someone, Stephanie turned around to see who it was. "He's cute, and it looks like he's coming over to talk to you."

"Don't get any ideas. He's the client I was telling you about. Adam."

"You didn't tell me was so good-looking."

"It didn't seem relevant."

Adam sauntered over to them. He was good-looking

and smart. Cheryl appreciated that he trusted her even when she didn't trust herself. After she introduced all of them, Adam took charge of the conversation immediately, asking them both about how they'd liked the party and finding out what they did. He was especially interested in Damon's art.

"I think I've seen some of your work around town," he said.

"Have you been to Liberty Bistro?" Damon had seemed so reserved before Adam joined the conversation, but as soon as Adam started talking about his art, he perked up.

Adam paused for a moment as if realizing something. "Did you paint that amazing mural?"

Stephanie shifted uncomfortably.

"That was me." Damon beamed.

"Have you seen that mural?" Adam turned to Cheryl.

She shook her head. "I've been meaning to eat there but haven't gotten around to it yet."

"We have to go. I'll treat you." Adam turned his attention back to Damon. "Hey, now that I have the artist here in person I have something to ask you."

"Go ahead."

Adam leaned forward like he was about to ask a very important question. "Is that mural a painting of the barista that used to work at the Starlight until not too long ago. I think her name was ..."

"Lisa." Damon finished his sentence and Stephanie stiffened.

"She's Damon's ex." Stephanie grabbed hold of his

hand.

"Really?" Adam glanced at Stephanie. "I'm sure he's painted some amazing pictures of you too."

"He hasn't." Stephanie's voice dropped.

"Not yet. I'm working on something now." Damon looked at her and smiled.

Surprise passed over her face. "I didn't know that."

"I've been keeping it a secret from you."

"I can't wait to see it," she said.

**

The silence in the car on the way back to her house was almost too much for Cheryl to bear. As he drove, Adam kept stealing expectant glances at her as her mind swirled with worry. She'd thought Day would be able to help her. She'd hoped someone with that much experience would've seen something like Cheryl was experiencing before. Instead, she gave her unremarkable advice and told her to start charging for people to communicate with their dead relatives. Cheryl wasn't interested in that. Yeah, she could use a better way to make money, but staying alive and sane were her top priorities right now.

Adam cleared his throat. "I talked to Day tonight."

"Did you?" Cheryl had noticed them chatting early in the evening. She'd wondered how much he'd told her before she'd even gotten to say anything to Day at all.

"Yeah, it was strange. I didn't realize she was a psychic when I first started talking to her. She was asking me about a book I was looking at."

"Really?"

"She thinks you're talented. She said you know what you're doing. You have a natural gift. You need to trust yourself more though." He pulled up to a stoplight. With the car still, he could get a good long look at Cheryl.

Her skin bristled under his gaze. "Talented?" She looked over at him. His blue eyes searching her face.

"That's what she said. She told me you're a great psychic and I'm in good hands with you." He smiled at her. His soft smile creased his face in all the best ways.

"I asked her about what I should do."

"What did she say?"

Cheryl shook her head. "Nothing really. She told me to burn some sage and start a new business."

Adam laughed. "A new business?" The car behind them beeped letting them know that light had turned green. The tires screeched as he sped away from the light.

"Things are tight for me these days. She says they don't have to be. She says I'm sitting on a gold mine."

"You are." He drummed the steering wheel as he drove. "You could do a lot of good with this new ability of yours. She's right."

"I don't know if that's what I want. All of this is kind of scary. I keep hoping it will stop."

"It might not."

Cheryl hadn't considered the possibility she might be stuck this way, seeing spirits forever. "If it doesn't I don't know what I would do. I want my life to go back to normal." She gave a little chirp of a laugh. "As normal as a professional tarot card reader's life could ever be." She cleared her throat. "I've been getting these strange phone calls. Did I tell you about them?"

He nodded. "A little, but you didn't go into much detail."

She clamped her mouth shut. A tear slipped down her face.

He looked over at her. "Why did you stop talking?"

She wiped the tear from her eye. "I don't want to tell you the same story twice. That's a problem I sometimes have."

"You're not doing me any favors by keeping all this bottled up. We're in this together now. Remember that. It's you and me against all the ghosts in the world ... or at least in this town."

She smiled, and more tears came spilling out. Stephanie had been the only one Cheryl had felt much of a connection with since leaving Carl. She had been careful not to let any other men in, but Adam was right. They had a connection now. It was them against everyone else because no one else she told seemed to understand, not even Stephanie. "I want this to all go away." While she did want these ghosts to go away, she was grateful for the time she was spending with Adam. He was so much more than she had expected.

"I'm ashamed to admit this, but I don't. I enjoy the time we've been spending together. Meeting you has been the best thing that's happened to me in a while. I don't like that you're scared, and this is so hard for you, but if none of it happened we probably would've never spoken."

Cheryl turned to look at him. Was he really saying what she thought he was saying? She had insisted on keeping this relationship professional, only because she was afraid of what she was feeling too. "I don't know what to say." She looked down at her lap, fiddling with the straps on her purse. She could feel his eyes on her. The car came to a stop. She looked out the passenger's window to see they were parked in front of her building.

"Nothing to say? That's a first."

She looked at him. Maybe for the first time, she really looked at him. The streetlight shone into the car; the soft glow just enough to fill the shadowing places. His questioning gaze tugged at her heart in a way that terrified her. The last time she'd felt that was when she and Carl started dating. Experience told her that feeling could only lead to a terrible place. Part of her wanted to jump out of the car and run away, but she didn't. Cheryl was through running away. "Don't get used to it. I'm not speechless often."

He nodded slowly. "I know."

"I've liked spending time with you too. I've been trying to keep this professional, but to be honest, it's hard. You are really ..." She paused, unsure of her words. "Nice." That sounded stupid, but it was out of her mouth already.

"Nice." His eyes twinkled. "Thanks."

She was relieved he didn't take it badly. Nice was a weak word. She meant something so much more. "You're welcome." She opened the car door. "Thanks for the ride. You went out of your way for me and ..." She bit her lip, trying to hold back her emotions. "That means a lot to me."

"I'm happy to help. You've helped me more than I could ever repay already."

She wiped her eye. How she wished she had a tissue. "You paid me for that."

"Not enough." He looked out the windshield for a moment. "I know we've been seeing a lot of each other recently, but I would like to see you again tomorrow if you have time."

"We could have our lunch meeting tomorrow," Cheryl suggested.

"You could make up for that dinner date you canceled."

"I'd like that." She stepped out of his SUV. Looking up the sidewalk, she checked for ghosts. There were none.

"Good. I'll see you tomorrow then." His eyes shifted to look at the front of her building and then back at her. "Will you be okay going up by yourself?"

"Yeah. I don't think there's anyone around right now. I don't feel anything at least."

He nodded. "Are you sure?"

"Yes." The word projected a confidence she didn't really have.

"Okay then. I guess this is goodnight." He looked at her like he had something else he wanted to say.

She waited, watching his mouth until she felt uncomfortable. "Goodnight."

He watched her walk up to the glass doors of her building. He was still watching as she stepped inside, her shoes clicking on the white tile. When she started up the stairs, she turned and could still see his car sitting at the curb. She wondered if he was watching her through the glass door or maybe he was just sitting there checking his phone. She didn't know when he pulled off, but when she checked out of the living room window of her apartment, he was gone. When she thought about him, her heart fluttered like a restless bird in a cage.

Chapter Twenty-One

CHERYL could hear her phone ringing in her bag. She half expected it to be Adam calling to make sure she had made it into her apartment all right, but when she looked at the screen, she saw it wasn't him.

"Hello, Sydney," she said into the phone.

"I hope it isn't too late to call you." The reception was bad. Sydney's voice sounded like she was caught in a jar.

"No. I was just getting home. Is something wrong?" Cheryl flipped the switch on the wall, washing the living room in bright white light. She was happy to talk to Sydney because she wasn't quite ready to be alone yet, even if she didn't want to admit that to Adam. How would she have looked if she'd asked him to come up with her? Talking to someone on the phone was not the same as having them there with her, but it was better than nothing.

"I don't know. I'm starting to think I'm losing my mind." Her voice quivered.

Cheryl stood up a little bit straighter. "What happened?"

Sydney didn't speak, but Cheryl could hear her breath over the phone, raspy and fast like she was recovering from a brisk run. "There's someone here."

"Who?"

"I can feel him ... them. I don't know. It all comes in flashes. I need your help." Her voice was clipped.

"Tell me where you are." Cheryl scrawled Sydney's address on a piece of paper. "I'll be right there." She grabbed her purse and ran out the door. She was on the sidewalk before she thought to call Adam.

"Are you okay?" he asked when he picked up the phone.

"Are you home yet?" She stood on the sidewalk looking in the direction he would've gone.

"I'm a few blocks from your place. I'm turning around. I'll be there soon." He hung up the phone before she got a chance to explain why she was calling.

Cheryl knew all she had to do was call Adam and he'd rush to her side. He'd said as much before, but she was still getting used to the idea. Thinking about what their relationship might become formed a knot in her chest.

She waited outside, leaning against the drab stucco wall of her apartment building. She looked at the sky, stars barely visible in the deep, inky blue. She replayed the phone calls she had gotten in her mind while she waited for him; the crackling, the childlike voice asking for help. She needed to figure out what clues were buried in them. Adam's SUV screeched around the corner and lurched to a stop in front of her. She ran to it pulling the door open and jumping inside.

"What's wrong?" he asked.

"It's not me. It's Sydney. I met her through the Spirit Guides Hotline. She's been getting the same calls as me. She needs help." Cheryl pulled the door closed and clicked on her seatbelt. "I didn't want to go alone, and I didn't know who else to call." She looked at him with pleading eyes.

"You don't have to explain. You can always call me. We're in this together, remember? We're a team."

A team. It sounded good to her. Part of her was tired of tackling life alone. Another part was still scared. She tried to push that part down, but it was always bubbling up.

"Where are we going?" he asked.

She unfolded the crinkled piece of paper in her hand and read the address to him. It wasn't far. As they rode there, she told him everything she knew about Sydney, the calls they'd both been getting, the ghost. He had heard some of it before but listened again, his face tense. When they pulled up in front of the building, they looked at each other.

"This is it." He raised an eyebrow at her.

"Thank you for coming with me."

He got out of the car. "Stop thanking me and come on." He strode confidently to the door.

Cheryl hopped out of the car and hurried after him. She had no idea what they were walking into. Neither of them did, but uncertainty didn't stop them.

They ran up the stairs to the third floor. Adam took them two at a time. Cheryl hiked up her long skirt to do the same. They rushed up the hall checking the numbers on each of the doors as they passed them. Hers was at the end, 336. The door was open a crack, inviting them in.

"Sydney?" Cheryl called through the opening in the door. They waited for an answer and when there wasn't any Adam eased the door open. It was eerily silent. Cheryl pressed herself against the wall. It was like they were police officers in a movie except neither of them had a gun and this was real life. "Sydney?" Cheryl called again as they took a few tentative steps inside. They exchanged looks, neither of them saying a word. The front hallway was cramped. Five pairs of shoes lay in a pile immediately next to the door. A selection of bags hung on a hook above the shoes. Framed black-and-white pictures of animals decorated the walls: a giraffe, an elephant, a zebra. "Sydney, it's Cheryl. I'm coming inside. I have a friend with me."

The thick carpeting cushioned their steps. A lamp was on in the living room. It sat in the corner behind the zebra-striped sofa. Both their eyes were drawn to the place where the light was coming from. Neither noticed Sydney at first. She sat in the overstuffed chair in the opposite corner of the room, her eyes open wide she sat perfectly still.

"Sydney!" Cheryl rushed over to her, but she didn't move.

"What's wrong with her?" Adam asked.

"I don't know. How would I know?" Cheryl reached out and grabbed Sydney's shoulder.

Sydney took a long wheezing inhale like she was coming up from the bottom of the ocean, her lungs expanding, her body shuttering to life.

Seeing her move made Cheryl's heart start beating again. "Are you all right?" Her words poured over Sydney who was now leaning forward in her chair, taking fast steady breaths. "What happened to you?"

Cheryl did not need to hear her answer because as soon as she asked the question, she could see what had happened. The ghost with the burn was there. His slender arms outstretched in front of him, he materialized next to her. Cheryl let go of Sydney, and as she tried to move away from him, fell into Adam who caught her.

"What's happening?" Adam asked.

Cheryl couldn't answer. She opened her mouth to speak, but it was like her voice had been pulled out of her. She felt Adam's arms around her, holding her up, resisting as she pushed herself back and back, trying to get away from the bald ghost. She went rigid when his skeletal hand made contact with her. His fingers curled around her slim neck. He opened his mouth, and Cheryl expected to hear the crackling sound from before. She braced herself for noise to pour over her, but a puff of smoke came out, a wispy white cloud spread cold across her cheeks. She coughed. Cheryl didn't know what Adam or Sydney was doing. She was vaguely aware of them, talking in the background. Adam was lowering her gently to the carpet as he spoke, but it was as if she was somewhere else watching all this happen. The ghost was the most important thing in the room. It was just her and him. That's all there was space for. As it came closer to her, his face radiated cold. Cheryl wondered if that was what death was, the absence of heat. His face, narrow and sharp, hovered only a few inches from hers. Every part of her recoiled. Her organs seemed to fold in on themselves. She felt like she might implode. She wanted to close her eyes. She wanted to be somewhere else, anywhere but there. But she was there, and she had to look. She looked deep into his eyes, and saw something she didn't expect, a well of pain.

"Help them," he said without moving his mouth. His thoughts bled into hers, spreading through her mind like fear. "I started it, but by the time I'd realized, it was already too late. I couldn't get to them in time. It was all my fault. Help them, and we will all be free." He looked deep into her eyes. Reflected in the empty black holes where his eyes should've been Cheryl saw a woman and a child on a bed. Flames rose around them licking the ceiling. "They don't know it's too late. Help them understand." The ghost vanished as quickly as he'd appeared relinquishing his hold on Cheryl. Her body went limp. Tears oozed from her eyes.

"Are you okay?" Adam and Sydney asked. Sydney stood over her and Adam crouched down next to her.

Fear leaked from her as she realized the pain she felt wasn't hers but belonged to the ghost who had been wracked with guilt for so long.

"You saw him too, didn't you?" Sydney asked.

Cheryl nodded. She sat up and looked at Adam whose eyes were soft with caring. "Did you?"

"I felt him more than I saw him. But when he did appear to me, it was only in flashes a few seconds at a time."

"It was never like that for me," Cheryl said, her voice weak. "He touched me."

"I didn't think that was possible," Adam said.

"It's possible. It's happened before." Cheryl remembered the feeling of his hand on her, the look on his face, that pain buried beneath the fear. Cheryl was beginning to feel like herself again. "Sydney, have you felt spirits anyplace else in this apartment?"

"The bedroom. Sometimes when I'm in bed I feel afraid, I can't explain why."

Cheryl started to stand, and Adam immediately began to help her up. She rushed into the bedroom. They were there. The woman and child Cheryl had just seen in the vision. Their faces smudged with soot, they cried out. Gathering themselves to the middle of the bed, they looked around in panic. "Help us. Help us!" they called out over and over.

Cheryl walked over to the bed. "I'm here to help you." Cheryl kept her voice calm and steady.

In unison they called out, the child clinging to the mother, burying her tear-streaked face in her mother's chest. The mother screamed in terror. "Are you the devil?" the mother asked.

Cheryl shook her head. "I'm no devil. I'm here to help you."

"Then get some water and put out this fire. It's burning us up. You should be burning too," the woman shrieked.

"The fire is already gone. Look at us." Cheryl gestured toward Adam and Sydney.

The woman's eyes were wide with confusion. "Don't just stand there, help us."

Cheryl walked closer to the bed. With each step, the woman backed up toward the headboard pressing her back against it and screaming. "You are the devil. Stay away from us."

Cheryl wanted to touch her, to calm her and take her

and her child out of this misery. She reached out her hand, and it passed through the woman's leg. She wondered how the ghost with the burn had been able to touch her. "I know you see fire all around you, but the fire isn't here. This is all over. It has happened already but you're living it, again and again."

"I don't know what you're talking about!"

"It doesn't make sense, but I need you to calm down."

The child took a phone from the bedside table and dialed a number. "Help us! Help us!" she called into the phone.

"How did you walk through the fire?" the woman yelled. "Can you get us out?"

Cheryl nodded vigorously. "Trust me."

The woman wasn't looking at her though. Her eyes were focused on the fire she saw behind Cheryl.

"Look at me." Spreading two fingers in a "V" shape, she pointed at both of her eyes.

The woman's gaze moved. She looked right at Cheryl. Her breathing was ragged. Sweat poured down her face.

"This already happened. It is over now. You don't have to relive it. You can stop."

The woman's focus kept drifting back to the fire.

Cheryl reached out her hand a second time and tried to touch the woman's shin. This time she made contact with something that didn't quite feel like flesh. It was like putting her hand through a cool mist. This movement got the woman's attention. It was as if a spell had been broken and the woman's cool eyes focused only on Cheryl's. The panic drained from her face.

"Who are you?" she asked.

It was such a simple question, yet Cheryl didn't know how to answer it. "It doesn't matter who I am. I'm here because someone wants me to give you a message."

"Who?" the woman asked.

"I don't know, but he says all of this was his fault. He tried to help you, but it was too late."

"Too late?" The woman looked down at her child and then around at the fire-filled room.

The child, still holding the phone receiver to her ear, looked up at her mother, confusion flickering across her face. "Someone will come to help us soon," the girl said.

"They can't," the woman said, an unnerving calm settled across her face. "It's already too late."

The child dropped the phone receiver on the bed and opening her mouth let out a blood-curdling wail.

Cheryl shrank back at the sound. She wanted to run away from the hopelessness of the scene.

"It will be okay," the mother said, looking down at the cherub-faced girl.

The girl stopped crying. Her body shook with muted sobs as she wiped away her tears with the back of her hand.

"That's right," Cheryl said. She'd broken through. "It's all over. You don't have to do this anymore. You can rest."

The woman looked down at her daughter's face and then up again at Cheryl. "But I wasn't ready."

"No one ever really is, but that doesn't matter. You'll be …" The words caught in Cheryl's throat because she wasn't sure if they were true. She took a deep breath and tried again. "You'll be fine. You'll both be fine."

A tear slid down the woman's cheek, and she pulled her daughter into her. The terror that had gripped them slipped away. As they began to fade like smoke, the woman looked up at Cheryl and mouthed the words, "Thank you."

CHAPTER TWENTY-TWO

ADAM was shaken. He didn't know if he would ever get used to seeing Cheryl speak to the dead. What happened that night in Sydney's apartment was, in many ways, the same as what he had seen happen in his own, but just before she went into the trance Cheryl was oddly calm. She'd looked at him, her dark eyes seeming to speak. "Catch me," they said.

He was ready. When her body went slack, he was there. He caught her beneath her arms and lowered her to the floor. The room was electric. Energy bounced off the walls as Cheryl lay there her mouth moving just a little, her voice barely a whisper.

Sydney had asked him what was happening, and he explained the best he could. No explanation was good enough.

Cheryl dozed against the passenger's side window as he drove. In the early morning hours, they had the street to themselves. Cheryl breathed heavily. Adam didn't know how she was able to sleep after what she'd seen. She'd described the scene to both him and Sydney when she finally woke, her eyes wild and hands flailing as she spoke. He could see she was spent even then, but the adrenaline of the moment had kept her going. By the time they'd gotten to the car all the mental exertion had caught up with her. She was asleep before he'd even pulled out of the parking spot.

Adam's world had unraveled a year ago. That first day he came home to the chain on the door his reality started melting into a world full of superstition and unbelievable stories. He'd thought there was no way life could get any stranger, but he hadn't met Cheryl yet. They'd walked into the unseen world of spirits together. When he'd asked her to help him get rid of the ghosts haunting his apartment, he never thought he'd willingly seek out another place where spirits were wreaking havoc. He found that if it meant spending more time with her, he'd do it again and again.

"We're here." He touched her shoulder gently.

Cheryl woke right away. Clutching her sack-like purse in her lap, she sat up straight and blinked a few times. "I must've dozed off."

"You needed the rest. That must've been exhausting." When it was all over Adam was relieved she sat up and started speaking again. Seeing her lying on the floor twitching scared him more than any ghost ever had.

"Yeah..." Cheryl looked out of the passenger window, her hand resting on the door handle. "Thanks for everything tonight. You didn't have to go with me, but I'm glad you did." She turned and looked at him again. She cracked the door, and the car was awash in white light that pushed the dark outside world away.

"Are you okay?" he asked, noticing her hesitation. He couldn't blame her for delaying getting out of the car. Secretly, he didn't want her to leave. He never did. That was why he came back to take her to the bookstore. That was why when she called him again he was more than willing to go to Sydney's house with her. It wasn't curiosity about the ghost or even the need to solve the problem anymore; it was about seeing her. He felt like he needed an excuse to do that.

Cheryl shrugged before pushing the door open a little bit more. "I guess I just don't want to be alone."

"You don't have to be."

She got out of the car. With the door open she started fishing through her bag.

He waited for her to say something and when she didn't, he did. "I could come up with you." He wondered if he was giving her the wrong idea. "I mean ..." He cleared his throat. "To make sure everything is okay in your place. In case that ghost shows up again or something." He knew, in reality, he couldn't do anything about ghosts. That was her department, but he could be there for her.

"I know what you meant." She pulled her ring of keys from her purse. "That would be nice. You wouldn't mind?"

He turned off the car and was getting out before answering. "Of course not," he said.

As they walked toward the door of the apartment building she hooked her arm into his. He thought about how they must look, like a couple coming home in the wee hours of the morning. Too bad there was no one out to see them.

Cheryl's cat meowed angrily as she put her key in the lock.

"Somebody misses you," Adam joked.

"He is so demanding." Cheryl pushed the door open and seemed to scoop the cat up into her arms in one fluid motion. The cat purred and nestled into her chest.

Adam reached over and petted the cat's soft head.

Cheryl cradled the cat against her as she walked from one room to the next. Adam followed close behind. He could see the rigidness of her body as she walked around the apartment, her back stiff, her neck turning this way and that, checking every corner.

"Everything seems fine." Adam settled into the sofa and put his car keys and wallet on the end table. He wondered about his own apartment and hoped it was as quiet as he had left it. The idea of the Butlers still being there was in the corner of his mind, but he did his best to put those thoughts aside.

"Do you want anything to drink?" She stood before him. The cat had twisted around and was climbing up onto her shoulder. Cheryl leaned forward letting him walk down her back before jumping off onto the floor with a solid thud.

"Some water would be good."

She disappeared into the kitchen, and he could hear the clink of glasses and the glug of water being poured. "Ice?"

"No thanks." When he was with Cheryl time was suspended. They shared their own reality that no one else could touch. He knew he couldn't stay away from the rest of the world forever. Time would move on, and if he wasn't careful, his reasons for seeing her would vanish. He didn't know what he would do without her. It was difficult for him to realize it wasn't that long ago that he hadn't known her at all. How strange to think he had a life before Cheryl.

She stood, fidgeting, and watching him drink his water. Her long, blue skirt grazed the top of her feet as she swayed absentmindedly from side to side.

"Don't stand there watching me. I'm here to help you feel better, and right now it looks like I'm making you uncomfortable."

"I just don't know what to do. Maybe this was a bad idea. I just want to go to sleep." She crossed her arms over her chest and swallowed hard.

"Don't worry about me. Go to bed. I'll sleep here on the couch, that way I'm just a few steps away if you need me."

She pursed her lips and gave a fast nod. "Okay." She went into her bedroom and came out with a pillow, a neatly folded slate-colored sheet, and a thin blanket. "You can use these." She set the bedding on the sofa next to him.

"Thank you."

"I'm sorry I don't have a sofa bed."

"No need to apologize."

She said good night and went back to the bedroom, closing the door behind her. Adam put his empty glass in the kitchen sink because he didn't know if the dishes in the dishwasher were clean or not. Then he stood in the living room for a minute, looking at the books on her shelves. It was as if she had shopped exclusively at the bookstore they had been at earlier that evening. Just about everything she owned had something to do with tarot, palmistry, or energy healing. He could hear her moving around in the next room but tried not to pay attention. He felt as though listening to her getting ready for bed was violating her privacy. Instead, he tried busying himself with his own thoughts. Each time those thoughts returned to Cheryl he'd change course again. He thought about work. He thought about how he had to get up extra early to go home and change before returning to the office. He thought about the Butlers.

He laid the sheet over the couch, slipped out of his shoes, and stood in front of the sofa, thinking about taking off his jeans. He knew he'd be more comfortable sleeping in his boxers but after a lot of consideration decided against it. Instead, he undid the button of his jeans and laid down on the couch.

Adam spent most of the night staring up at the ceiling. He wondered if Cheryl was sleeping but dared not check. The night floated by, and when the first beams of light streamed in through the living room window, he sat up and put on his shoes. He would have to leave to get home in time to shower and change before going to work. When he told Cheryl he was leaving, she was still asleep, her body twisted in the sheet, her hair a mess of tangles around her face. She was so lovely it was hard for him not to lean over and kiss her.

"I have to go home now," he said.

She grunted. He didn't know if she was responding to him or someone in a dream.

Adam had been so full of ideas that night that he

hardly slept. They danced in his head until the best one got caught like an ant in glue. It was perfect. It had taken all his willpower not to wake Cheryl right away and tell her about it. He would tell her when he saw here that afternoon. She would think it was as wonderful as he did. He was sure of it.

When Adam's telephone rang just before lunchtime he was afraid it was Cheryl canceling on him again. The muscles in his face tightened. When he picked up the phone, he saw it was his sister.

"Hey, Jules," he said. "Do you need me to watch the monsters again?"

"They are monsters. Chloe has been ..." She sighed deeply. "Sometimes I get so scared. What's going to happen as she grows up? If she's this hard for me to manage now, what will she be like when she's sixteen?" There was some noise in the background. "Do your work?" she said. Her stern voice was muffled. Adam could hear Chloe's high-pitched voice in the background but couldn't tell what she was saying. "No, Chloe. You have to finish your math first." Chloe's complaining continued, but got quieter, like she was moving away from the phone. "You have fifteen more minutes to finish it." Adam heard a door close. "Adam?"

"Yeah." He knew his niece was difficult, but he never saw that side of her. "It sounds like you have your hands full."

Jules lowered her voice. "I have to do what I can now before she gets too old." She sighed again. "Enough about my problems. That's not why I called."

"I thought you called because you needed advice from your wise younger brother."

"No." She didn't laugh. "When you spent the night, you seemed anxious. I know that was ages ago now and I should have called you sooner, but I've been so busy with the kids."

"I know you're busy. Homeschooling Chloe is like having two full-time jobs."

"Tell me about it."

"I'm a big boy. I can take care of myself." When they were young Jules always looked out for him. He was an unusually small child, and the other children in school teased him often. Jules was always there to stick up for her younger brother.

"I know, but I'm family. I want to make sure you're okay." She was quiet for a moment. "So, are you?"

"Yeah. I was having a hard time when I stayed over, but I it's all working out." Adam had been getting to the point where he was afraid he'd end up living with those ghosts forever. Now his life was so different. "I've got some exciting plans."

"Really? What?"

He wanted to tell Jules about Cheryl and his business idea, but Jules was as practical as he once thought he was. If he told her he was in love with a psychic and considering opening a business with her, Jules would freak out. He wouldn't blame her either. "I want it to be a surprise. As soon as I get it all up and running, I'll tell you."

"Okay." Jules was always good at letting him take his

time with things.

"You used to be into looking at our family history, didn't you?"

"I still do that when I have time. Why?"

"Are there any missing links, like a great great-grandfather maybe?"

"Actually, yeah. We have a great great-grandmother, Patricia Spector, who was a single mother. That was rare back then. Funnily enough, she'd moved from Florida with her infant son up north to Michigan. Now we're both back down in Florida again. Anyway, she was a widow who never remarried. No matter how hard I look I can't find any marriage records, and there's no father listed on her son's birth certificate. I think she was an unmarried mother. That was a real scandal back then. Why do you ask?"

Adam smirked. "I think the child's father was Charles Butler."

"Who? How would you know that?" she asked.

"Just look him up, and you'll see what I'm talking about."

"Since when are you interested in family history?"

"I'm interested in a lot of things you don't know about." Adam could hear Chloe in the background again. She was calmer this time.

"I have to go, but you have to tell me what you're planning next time we talk." Chloe's voice was getting louder.

"I will. Remember to look up Charles Butler."

"Will do. Love you. Bye." She hung up.

Adam looked at the time on his phone. It was almost

lunchtime. He had to get going. He didn't want to be late for his meeting with Cheryl.

CHAPTER TWENTY-THREE

CHERYL wandered into the living room still groggy from sleep. "Adam!" she called his name several times. Disappointment settled into her when she realized he wasn't there. She stood looking at the sheets and blanket, neatly folded and placed at the end of the sofa. She hadn't even heard him leave. He probably didn't want to disturb her when he left for work, but she still felt hurt he hadn't said goodbye. The first day Adam asked her for a reading, Cheryl never would've thought she'd end up having feelings for him.

She eyed the phone on the table next to the sofa suspiciously, hoping it wouldn't ring today. Part of her wanted to get rid of the phone altogether, but she knew she couldn't. She still needed it for work. She sat down and started sorting through the stack of mail on the coffee table. It had been piling up for days. Ignoring it didn't make her bills go away, and she was pretty sure she didn't have enough money in the bank to cover them all.

She picked up a deck of her favorite tarot cards and

lowered herself to the floor to give herself a reading. The future seemed a lot more certain, but it never hurt to ask the cards. She did the same simple three card layout she did for herself most mornings. She turned the cards over slowly hoping they would give her good news: The Page of Pentacles, Nine of Cups, and Four of Pentacles. She sat on the floor with her legs crossed looking at the cards, her eyes welling up with tears. She couldn't think of a better spread for that day. The cards told her what she already knew herself. What had happened in these few short weeks had changed her life. She was determined to study further so she could help the spirits however she could. Day was right. She had a gift, and her greatest success in life would come from sharing it. A mixture of fear and joy fluttered in her stomach. Her life was going to be completely different. There was no arguing with that. She needed to embrace this new gift.

"Life is about to turn around," she said to Beau who rolled onto his back in the beam of light that cascaded in through the living room window exposing the downy fur on his belly.

Cheryl was surfing the Internet and eating a bowl of cereal when her telephone binged letting her know she had a text message. The text was from Adam reminding her about their lunch date. Of course she remembered. She couldn't wait to see him and tell him about what she had discovered.

Cheryl was free until lunch, so she decided to find a spirit to help. She was through running away from the dead.

Now she would pursue them. She didn't have to go far before she saw the man in the suit she had seen a few nights before. He leaned against the brick building next to her apartment holding his hat in his hand and watching the people walk past. Cheryl squared her shoulders and took a few deep breaths before walking up to him. Aware of what she would look like to everyone else when she talked to him, she waited until the sidewalk was relatively empty before she said anything.

"Excuse me, but I've seen you around, and I was wondering if you need any help." She leaned in, trying to speak as quietly as possible.

His eyes widened in shock as he looked at her. "Are you talking to me?" He pointed at his chest.

Cheryl nodded.

"You can see me?" He turned to face her and put his hat on his head.

"Yes." Cheryl made sure her answer was as clear as possible. "My name is Cheryl. What's your name?"

"Sam Hayes." His eyes lit up when he said his name. His narrow face, all angles and points, radiated with a happiness Cheryl had not seen on anyone before. He held out his hand to shake.

"We can't shake hands." Cheryl was very much aware of the group of men in business suits walking by her as she spoke. None of them seeming to notice she was talking to herself.

"Of course not." The man shoved his hand into the pocket of his black pinstriped pants.

"I was wondering if you realized you are..." Cheryl

tried to think of a delicate way to put this, but after some consideration decided it was best to be straightforward. "Dead."

The man laughed. "Deader than a doornail. I'm more than aware of that. I've been this way long enough."

"Why don't you move on then?"

"The question of the century." The man stood up straight and rocked forward onto his toes and then back onto his heels. "I liked living too much. I wasn't ready to call it quits when they decided it was my time."

His answer didn't feel right to her. "How come every time I've seen you you've been so sad, then?"

The man shrugged. "Not sad. Just lonely."

"Don't you think you'd be happier someplace else. I mean, less lonely." Traffic was picking up on the sidewalk again. Cheryl did everything she could to try to push her embarrassment away.

Jonathon seemed distracted. He honed in on something across the street. "I have to go."

He vanished before Cheryl could say anything else. When Cheryl turned to see what he'd been looking at she saw Betty, the elderly woman that had told her about Adam's ghosts. Her back hunched, she walked slowly up the sidewalk using a bright pink cane to steady herself as she went. Sam appeared walking next to her, his hand resting on the small of her back. Cheryl hurried across the street to them. "Betty!" she called.

The woman stopped and leaned forward, resting her weight on the cane she looked over at Cheryl. Her watery blue eyes sparkled with recognition. "Now this is a coincidence. Are you ready to give me my reading?"

"I didn't know if you'd recognize me." She jogged over to her, the strap of her purse slipping from her shoulder, she hiked it up.

"My body is giving out, but my mind is still all there. Who could forget a girl as stunning as you?" She smiled revealing a row of plastic-looking white teeth.

Cheryl looked at Sam who crinkled his forehead at her and shook his head. Then she looked back at Betty who was staring at her with quizzical eyes.

"What are you looking at?" she asked Cheryl.

Cheryl shook her head. "Nothing. I'm just so glad to see you out and about."

"I'm always out and about. That's the only way I can stay sane these days. Heaven knows I can't stay cooped up inside all day. I like to have my daughter-in-law drop me off downtown, so I can go for a little stroll before I meet the girls at the coffee shop. She always acts like she's worried I'll get lost or break a hip. She's a nervous girl." Betty spat out a dry cough. "She'd have you thinking I was made of glass and had a brain the size of a pea. I need to get out and walk around. It keeps me healthy."

"It sure does." Cheryl noticed how Sam looked down at the woman lovingly the entire time she spoke. "I'd love to give you a reading. Would you feel comfortable coming up to my apartment for it? I live across the street there." She pointed at the drab stucco building across the street.

Betty didn't think about it for very long. "I'd love to go to your apartment for a reading."

Cheryl hooked her arm in Betty's, and they crossed the

street.

"Your apartment is nice," Betty said as she settled herself on the sofa. She scooted back on the couch, so her feet didn't touch the ground. Her clean white sneakers hovered a good six inches from the floor. "It's all so very Bohemian, just as I imagined."

After clearing off the coffee table, Cheryl pulled out her tarot cards. She gave them a little shuffle then passed them to Betty and asked her to do the same. Sam paced back and forth in the living room in front of them, rubbing his neck like he was nervous. Cheryl wanted so badly to tell him he had no reason to worry but knew if she started talking to invisible people, Betty might feel unsafe.

The reading went well. The cards said all that needed to be said. They were so on target Cheryl wondered if Sam had manipulated them somehow. The words poured out of her with no effort at all. It all made sense. She told Betty she'd lived a good and full life and she was being looked after by someone on the other side who loved her very much.

Betty pulled a tissue from the pocket of her pale pink jeans and dabbed her eyes. "I feel him all around me especially now. Sometimes, I'm not sure if what I'm feeling is real or not."

Sam stopped pacing and rushed over. He joined them on the sofa, sitting on the other side of Betty. She turned her head looking right into his eyes, and for a moment it was as if Betty could see him too. "You must think I'm a foolish old woman."

"Not at all," Cheryl said. "We have spirits all around

us."

"Maybe all of this means my time is almost up."

Cheryl started to speak, but Betty continued.

"Don't feel bad for me. I'm an old lady, and to be honest, I'm getting tired. Maybe feeling the deceased around you is what happens right before you are going to join them."

"I don't know." Cheryl hoped what she'd said wasn't true because she wasn't ready to leave this world yet. She had a lot to do. She was still young. That was how she thought of herself at least. The idea of dying and never seeing her friends or Adam chilled her heart. "I hope you're wrong because I've been surrounded by the dead and I'm not ready to die yet. There are too many things I haven't done." She could feel her eyes growing hot with tears at the thought. "There are too many things I haven't said."

Betty put her cool hand on Cheryl's forearm. The skin on Betty's hand was soft and fragile. "Well, say them. You aren't going to live forever. You have to live life while it's here for you."

Cheryl looked at Betty and then at Sam who said, "You know she's right."

Cheryl gave a weak laugh. Now ghosts were giving her advice. She sniffled. "I know." Life was too short for her to keep holding back. That was a lesson she should've learned when Carl almost killed her. Even though she would always remember that day, she'd forgotten the message it carried. She wiped the tears from her eyes.

"Look at us," Betty said. "We're both blubbering messes. Is this normal for a tarot reading?"

"No," Cheryl said. "I'm usually much more composed. I'm sorry for falling apart. I've been having an interesting few weeks."

"You don't have to apologize to me. I've seen and heard it all." Betty looked down at the cards on the table. "It's funny how a deck of cards could know so much about me."

"It is." Cheryl gazed down at the cards too. She realized she hadn't given them the respect they deserved in the past. Sure, they were just a tool, but they were a tool that had served her so well for so long. She hadn't realized it before. She'd taken it all for granted. She wasn't going to do that anymore.

Betty looked at the silver watch she wore on her thin wrist. "I have to go. I'm meeting the girls at the coffee shop. I don't want to be late."

Cheryl escorted Betty outside. "That was a lovely reading. Thank you so much. How much do I owe you?" She reached into her handbag with a shaky hand.

"That one was on the house. You can pay me next time." Betty tried to protest and shove a five-dollar bill into her hand, but Cheryl wouldn't allow it. "Just give me a big tip next time," she said.

"Thank you," Betty said before turning to walk up the street.

"Thank you for not telling her," Sam said. "I don't want to upset her."

Cheryl wanted to tell him she didn't think knowing about him would upset her. Frankly, Cheryl thought it might do just the opposite, but she couldn't say any of that now, not without Betty noticing.

Cheryl watched Sam and Betty stroll up the road together, hoping that, one day, someone would love her as much as he seemed to love Betty.

CHAPTER TWENTY-FOUR

ADAM had picked up his phone to text Cheryl when he saw her rushing through the door. He stood, but she was already making a beeline for him.

"Sorry I'm late," she said over the buzz of the restaurant. The strap of her large purse slipped from her shoulder, spilling its contents all over the scuffed brown tile floor.

Adam rushed over to help her clean it up. A thin waitress with mousy-brown hair pulled up into a messy bun stooped down to help also. She examined each object before handing it to Cheryl: a blue stone, a satchel of tarot cards, lip balm.

When they finished cleaning up her collection of odds and ends they all stood.

"Thank you," Cheryl said to the waitress who had already walked away. She looked at Adam sheepishly and shrugged.

Adam took her by the elbow and guided her to their table. "You sure know how to make an entrance."

"Yeah right." She gripped her bag at the top, holding the opening together. "I just need to get a better bag, but this one has sentimental value."

"Really? Why?" She lowered herself into the chair he'd pulled out for her and placed her bag on the floor beside her feet.

"It's a long story, and it's not really what I wanted to talk about today."

Adam raised an eyebrow. He hadn't known she wanted to talk about anything at all. This lunch was his idea. Even though he was bursting at the seams to tell her about his brilliant plan for them both, she had piqued his curiosity. "What did you want to talk about then?"

She looked nervously around the crowded restaurant. Every table was full, and people were waiting at the door to be seated. "Let's order first." She opened the menu and started scanning the items. "I hate going out to eat during lunchtime on a weekday. I feel like everyone's in a hurry. They all have someplace to go, and I need to hurry up too. I don't like to feel rushed when I'm eating."

"I have to get back to work too." Adam was painfully aware of the time. They only had a little less than an hour. He hoped it was enough time to make his case. He kept reminding himself they could always talk again later, but it was difficult to ignore the feeling of urgency rising in his chest.

After they ordered their food, Adam watched Cheryl fidget with the silverware for a few moments, hoping she would tell him what she wanted to talk about. Growing tired of waiting he finally spoke. "So, do you want to go first or should I?"

"I didn't realize you had something to say." She looked up from the fork she had been tapping on the table.

"This lunch was my idea."

"What did you want to say?" She put the fork down and folded her hands on the table in front of her.

Adam cleared his throat. "Okay, I guess I'll go first. I've been thinking about your new abilities and..." Adam realized he didn't know how he was going to explain his idea to Cheryl. He wanted her to say yes, but he had been so excited about what could happen, he forgot to come up with a plan. "You know you said you're terrible with the business side of things."

She nodded in confirmation.

"Well, I'm pretty good at that stuff. What you can do is so amazing that—"

She cut him off. "I think we're thinking along the same lines. I've been trying to fight this all the time when I should be accepting it. It's a blessing, right?"

"Yeah, it is," he said. "Why not take advantage of it." After he spoke, he thought it might have sounded bad. "I mean why not use it to help people and help yourself at the same time." What he said still didn't seem to come out right, but she was already talking again.

"I gave myself a reading this morning, and it said I should embrace this. Day was right when she told me this is what I need to be doing. I can keep doing the tarot. I still have people who want readings, but this should be my main thing. I don't want to be on TV or anything, like the Long Island Psychic. To be honest, I think she's a bit of a con artist. I want to help people. I don't want to be famous. It would be nice not to have to worry about paying my bills though." She bit her lip and thought for a moment. "The main problem I see is that the people don't necessarily come to me for help, the ghosts do. I can't get ghosts to pay me."

"There are people experiencing hauntings, like Sydney and me. We can help them. I mean, you can help them. I guess I'll just be helping you."

She laughed. "You can help me, help them."

"Yeah." Adam was so glad she thought this was a good idea too that he wanted to jump up from the table and kiss her.

"But what if I go to see them and the ghost isn't there. What if I can't produce results?"

"We'll just charge the people we help. I would go with you to the jobs, of course, as your assistant." He thought of the way she looked when she encountered the ghost at Sydney's apartment. Her eyes rolled back in her head, and she collapsed on him. It would've been terrible if he hadn't been there to catch her. He couldn't let that happen. The last thing he wanted was for her to get hurt doing this.

"I never thought about needing assistance."

"Trust me, you do. You didn't see what happened at Sydney's."

"That doesn't happen all the time," she said. "I think it only happens when the ghost's needs are particularly strong. Usually, talking to them is like having a conversation with anyone else."

He wasn't going to compromise on this. He needed to be there to make sure she was safe. "I'll be there for the rare times it isn't like having a conversation with anyone else then."

"You're probably right."

The waitress brought their food over. "Do you need anything else?" she asked.

They both shook their heads.

Adam was starving. He hadn't had time to eat breakfast that morning. His hamburger was exactly what he needed. He started to feel better as soon as the food hit his stomach. "So, it looks like we're going into business together."

"Yes, it most definitely does." Cheryl's face shone with joy.

Adam wanted to think she was happy because this business idea meant they would keep seeing each other.

Cheryl had a special gift that needed to be shared, but secretly, he wasn't ready to stop seeing her. She needed him even though she didn't seem to realize it yet. If he could stay in her life a little longer, she'd start to see it, like he had. He never thought this odd talkative woman would capture his heart, but somehow, during all the craziness, she had. No matter what the future had in store for them, he felt like he could tackle it with her.

CHAPTER TWENTY-FIVE

EVERYTHING was coming together. Adam had given her exactly what she needed, a partner, and she didn't know how to express her gratitude.

The chattering of the crowd in the restaurant echoed on the walls. Her pasta was the most delicious food she'd ever tasted. The tang of the sauce and the spring of the noodles were like eating pure joy. She sat on the edge of her chair as she and Adam traded ideas. It was like an exciting game of ping-pong. Her body rumbled with excitement thinking about all the possibilities. Adam radiated enthusiasm. He was obviously tired. He had bags under his eyes from going to sleep so late the night before. Cheryl doubted he slept well on her sofa. It was too lumpy and uncomfortable, but he hadn't complained. She watched his mouth move as he talked and wondered what it would be like to kiss him. She kept reminding herself he wasn't a client anymore, so these thoughts were fine. They were probably fine before too. Rules were made to be broken or something like that. That's what her brother used to say.

That was why he ended up a drug addict with no real job, but Cheryl didn't want to dwell on the bad parts. She wanted to remember the good bits, like how her brother would laugh so hard at his own jokes he'd double over, holding his stomach. That was just one of the good bits. Life was so full of good bits, especially now. Adam was becoming one of those good bits. He was as good as finding a twenty-dollar bill on the street or getting a call from a long-lost friend.

"I have a lot of plans," he said. "I don't think there is anyone in this area who does this. We'll have the market cornered, and you are so good at it."

"I don't know how much demand there will be." There she was being a downer again. At her core, she was kind of a disappointment, and she wanted him to be prepared.

"It will take a little while to get a good reputation, but it will happen. I know it. We don't have to stay around here. We could travel."

"Traveling would be fun." What Cheryl wanted to say was traveling with you sounds like fun, but she wasn't sure how appropriate it would be to say something like that to her new business partner.

"Traveling with you sounds like fun."

Everything in the room seemed to stop. Had he just said what she thought he'd said? It was as if she had been dropped into a vacuum and there was only her and him. Her face began to flush. She took a few deep breaths. "Yeah, I bet traveling with you will be a lot of fun."

"I hope you realize all this is just an elaborate excuse to spend more time with you."

244

Cheryl's heart thumped. Could he read her mind suddenly? She'd thought she was the only one with psychic gifts. "You don't have to go into business with me to do that. All you have to do is ask me out."

He held out his hand gesturing to the restaurant. "Didn't I already do that?"

Cheryl smiled. "I guess you have." The energy between them shifted so quickly Cheryl felt like she could feel the air in the room heat up.

"I plan on spending a lot more time with you too," he said.

"Good."

Cheryl's face flushed as he stood and leaned across the table toward her. The front of his white shirt brushed the top of his half-eaten hamburger staining the fabric. As if driven by an unseen force she half stood too. She could feel her orange shirt making contact with the tomato sauce on her plate as she leaned into him. She didn't care. She had other shirts. She'd thought about kissing him so many times and never thought it would happen in a crowded restaurant during lunch on a Wednesday over a table of food, but it was perfect. For the first time in a long time Cheryl was at a loss for words.

Epilogue

Spanish moss swung from the low-hanging branches of the oak tree. They'd seen pictures of the house online, but nothing could've prepared them for what it looked like in real life. It was the monstrosity of the neighborhood complete with gargoyles and vast Roman columns. Built by a wealthy eccentric more than a hundred years ago, the house had been left to rot over the years. They didn't have to go inside to know it was haunted. Even people who didn't believe in such things would've guessed it was. The new owners of the place wanted to restore it to its former glory, but they'd run into a lot of snags along the way.

"I think we have ghosts in our house," Ms. Flannery had told Adam on the phone the previous week. "Every time I say that I feel like I must be going crazy, but I swear I'm not."

She didn't have to explain herself to Adam. He already knew.

As they stood at the end of the wooded driveway looking at the old mansion, Cheryl rubbed the lapis stone in her pocket. She'd left her old purse and tarot cards at home. Over time, she'd realized she didn't need them. The ghosts came directly to her. She didn't need tools.

They'd settled on their last names as a company name. Blake and Kennedy Paranormal Investigators. The name had no pizzaz, but it was descriptive enough, and that was all that mattered. Cheryl decided it wasn't that important anyway but made it clear she might want to change it in the future. The most important thing was helping the ghosts and helping the people who were having problems with them. As long as she did that it didn't matter what they named their company.

"Are you ready?" Adam said.

Cheryl never felt particularly ready, but she was willing to try and that was as ready as she needed to be. "Yeah," she said, brushing the hair out of her eyes.

Adam leaned down to kiss her, and she relaxed. She'd been single for so long she'd almost forgotten what love could be like. With Adam, everything was better. She never thought that could be the case with any man. "You'll do great," he said. "You always do."

Even though she could feel the dark energy seeping from the house, she believed him. That was the first step to conquering whatever waited for them beyond the house's large oak door. Linking her arm in his they walked up the front walk together. This would be their first job as Suncoast Paranormal and Cheryl hoped it would not be their last.

Note From the Author

Do you want to know what happens to Cheryl and Adam next? I wrote a short story about their first job as paranormal investigators. It's called The Flannery Haunting and you can get it for free by visiting the site below.

http://www.lovelynbettison.com/get-the-suncoast-paranormal-short-story/

About the Author

Lovelyn Bettison writes speculative fiction with a multicultural cast. She lives in Florida with her husband, son, and dog. Go to her website to sign up for her newsletter where you can get special offers and be the first to find out about her latest books.

LovelynBettison.com

BOOKS BY LOVELYN BETTISON

UNCOMMON REALITIES SERIES

Perfect Family
The Box
Flying Lessons

STARLIGHT CAFE SERIES

The Barista
The Psychic
The Widow

ISLE OF GODS SERIES

The Vision
The Escape
The Memory